RAY

Riding Hard Book 7

JENNIFER ASHLEY

JA / AG Publishing

Chapter One

The cowboy was muscular, solid, and stepped right in her way. Drew never saw him over the pile of paint buckets, drywall joint compound, and aluminum duct tubing half sliding out of her arms, until it was too late.

She ran smack into him.

The aluminum made a hell of a lot of noise as it clattered to the floor of the hardware store. The drywall joint compound followed, the bag splitting, white powder bursting over Drew's jeans, the floor, and down the entire front of the cowboy, whose firm body was like a wall.

"Damn it," Drew whispered as she scrambled for her items, dropping more in the process. "Damn it. *Damn* it."

Mr. Fuller, the owner of the store, popped out of another aisle and viewed the mess with dismay. He'd kick her out, and then Drew would have to search far and wide for another store that had the mountain of things she needed so she and her daughter could sleep in rooms not falling apart.

Two large hands righted the broken bag of compound and set it against a shelf then reached for the tubing.

"Careful now." The cowboy's voice was as large as the rest of him.

Drew risked a glance at his face, her own hotter than fire, and her breath deserted her.

If she had to run into someone, why did it have to be the best-looking man she'd ever seen in her life? He had dark hair under a black cowboy hat, a hard face softened by a few lines about his mouth, and wide shoulders with a sliver of chest showing above his now powder-coated black shirt.

His eyes arrested her most of all. They were green, a shade of jade, which sparkled in contrast to his dark hair and tanned skin.

Drew must have spent a full minute staring at his eyes. Not that she wasn't aware of the rest of his body—as rock-hard and well-formed as an artist's sculpture.

"Sorry." Drew realized she needed to say something. "Didn't see you. You okay?"

She pulled her gaze down to the huge splotch of white powder that started at his chest and fully dusted the front of his jeans.

"Damage isn't permanent," the cowboy said. "Let me help you with that. Hey, Craig—you got a cart or a trolley or something back there?"

Drew heard someone crashing around, and then a man not many years younger than the cowboy came around the corner with a flat dolly. The young man was Craig Fuller, son of the owner, who'd helped her find the right pipes and pointed her to the drywall section not ten minutes ago.

"Sorry about that. Should have given you this earlier." Craig joined the cowboy in loading Drew's things onto the dolly. He looked critically at the remains of the bag. "I'll get you some more joint compound." He dashed away.

Drew's defenses softened. She was a total stranger here and had heard that small-town residents, especially in rural Texas, shut strangers out. But these two were gallantly picking up her mess, helping her without a word.

"I'll pay for the broken bag," she said quickly.

"No, I will," the cowboy said. "I ran into you."

Drew shook her head. "I ran into *you*."

"Well, we can debate about that for a while, but I'll win, so don't bother." The cowboy took a card out of his wallet and passed it to Mr. Fuller. "Add it to my order."

Mr. Fuller didn't give Drew time to debate. He took the cowboy's credit card and moved to the register at the front. Craig headed there too, hefting the new bag of compound to show her it was waiting for her.

"What you need all this stuff for anyway?" the cowboy asked. "Looks like you're repairing walls, plumbing, *and* electricity." He turned over the coils of wire and switch boxes, as well as wire strippers and pliers. "Have a shack you're fixing up?"

"Sort of." Drew took a breath, tamping down her irritation, her anger, her near despair.

Before she could explain, Craig called down the aisle, "The old Paresky house. This here's Drew, Paresky's granddaughter."

The cowboy's gaze flickered with interest. "Really? The Paresky ... uh ... place?"

Drew's eyes narrowed. "You were going to say *dump*, weren't you?"

The cowboy's cheeks reddened. "Well ..."

"Don't worry." Drew let out an exasperated sigh. "It *is* a dump. But it's my dump now."

The cowboy looked Drew up and down with a gaze that

would be considered rude—even homicidally so—in Chicago. But here, everyone stared at Drew like this. She was new, an oddity, and yet, she had roots in Riverbend.

On the other hand, she'd never been to this town, let alone the state. While Drew had been curious about her grandparents' small town in a vague way, her life hadn't given her time to think deeply about it.

She'd found what was known as the Hill Country and Riverbend itself to be beautiful. Refreshing. Calm. But she was already getting tired of being an object of curiosity.

"Thanks so much for helping," Drew said to end the conversation. "And sorry I ran into you."

She grabbed the handle of the dolly, trying to plow it around the cowboy and back toward the register. The wheels stuck and went every which way, explaining the clattering she'd heard before.

The cowboy grasped the bar, brushing her hands with his warm ones. A flare of sudden heat shot through Drew, one she quickly suppressed, but her heart hammered.

He expertly maneuvered the dolly through the aisle, turned it in the open space at the end, and pushed it to the register. "There's a trick to them," he said when she caught up.

Drew took out her credit card—which would reach its max very soon—and paid for the rest of the supplies. She winced when she saw the total.

The cowboy stood close to her, leaning on the dolly as Craig set the purchases on it after his father rang them up. The cowboy's gaze stayed on Drew's face as she slid the card back into her wallet.

Without a word, he pushed the dolly outside for her and around the corner to the dirt lot where the customers parked for the feed store. He went directly to her small car, probably figuring from the process of elimination which was hers. Of course, it was the only *car* in the lot—all the other vehicles were pickups.

"No way you're getting all this stuff in your bitty trunk," the cowboy said, rightly so. "How about I haul it in my truck?" He gestured to the big black Ford 250 parked near the hay barn in the back. "I know where the Paresky place is —on Ranch Road 2889, right?"

"Yes." Drew swallowed. "But I can't let you … I mean, it's nice, but I don't even know you."

One thing to have a handsome stranger help her in the store, another to have him follow her to her house. Or precede her. Drew still wasn't sure of her way around.

"I'm Ray." The cowboy stuck out his hand for her to shake. "Ray Malory. Everyone knows me."

She took his hand, finding his grip hard, fingers strong, his touch fanning the heat she'd tried to suppress.

"Drew Paresky," she managed, withdrawing with difficulty. "Oh, right, you already know that."

"How do you do?" The twinkle in his eyes told her the formality amused him. "Only makes sense—my truck's plenty big enough for all this. I'll meet you out there and unload it for you, then I'll leave you be. All right?"

What could she say but, "Sure." Turn down help when she needed it? A large vehicle that easily held what would take hers three trips to haul?

If he turned out to be an ax murderer, she could always lock the door and call the cops … if the locks on the doors actually worked, and she could find a cell phone signal.

Better idea—she'd get there before him and instruct him to leave everything in the driveway. Drew could barricade his way to the house and her daughter inside it if necessary.

The trouble was, Ray took off before Drew could get into her car and start it. He knew exactly where the old bed and breakfast lay in its derelict heap, and headed there without hesitation.

Drew caught up to Ray's pickup after he'd turned onto the road to the B&B. On maps this route that snaked through the hills was marked as the 2889, sometimes labeled as FM— Farm to Market, sometimes RR—Ranch Road. The name changed every mile and a half for no reason Drew could discern.

She caught up to Ray only because he slowed to wait for her. The posted speed was fifty, and when Drew reached Ray's truck, he was creaking along at about thirty. When she waved at him from behind, he sped up, taking off in a roar.

Drew's car was a small Toyota sedan that had seen better days. Not bad for driving around—and parking in—a city and its burbs, but it was out of place in this vast land of endless and very straight highways.

Only one other vehicle passed them—another pickup— going the other way, west into town. The driver lifted a hand to Ray, and Ray waved back.

Did they know each other? Or just being courteous?

Was she kidding? Everyone knew everybody in River-bend, at least it seemed so. She was the only incongruity, the new and intriguing fixture they gaped at. As out of place as her car.

Ray slowed and pulled onto the dirt road that led between fence posts—no fence or gate—to the B&B. She followed the lane between two hills that sloped down to a wide meadow. The land was deep green now, but Mrs. Ward, the lady who owned the diner, had told her that in spring, the hills would be purple with bluebonnets.

The B&B was a long, dilapidated two-story house situated in the curve of a drive. Trees lined the house's west side, which would give it shade in the heat of the day, but the rest of the house faced a view—a beautiful one—of gentle hills and vast sky. The road lay hidden behind the folds of land, giving the whole place the illusion of isolated splendor.

Ray halted the truck near the garage—a two-story standalone building with rooms upstairs. Thank heavens for those rooms, which was where Drew's grandfather had been living. They were the only ones habitable on the whole property.

The water and electricity had been disconnected when Drew had arrived, and it had taken her a long time of arguing and producing deeds to the property before the county's electric company would turn the power back on. They were surprised she hadn't wanted to use the generator. For water, the property had a well and a pump, which Drew hadn't understood how to work. A sullen man from the county had to come out and show her. In Chicago, you paid a bill and someone you never saw flipped a switch.

Drew jumped out of the car as Ray hauled down the tailgate of his truck. Instead of unloading, he leaned on the truck bed, tilted back his cowboy hat, and studied the main house.

Drew's heart sank as she looked it over with him. The porch sagged, the steps to it half gone. Windows were broken and boarded up, or had simply been left gaping without glass. The front screen door was long gone—she'd found the hinges in place but the screen door in the grass in the back.

That was nothing to the peeling paint, fallen gutters, missing shutters, and electric wires hanging like spaghetti—thankfully hooked up only to the generator that was shut down, out of fuel.

Inside was fading or moldy wallpaper—wherever it was still on the walls—rusty plumbing fixtures, outdated and non-working appliances, rotted floors, window air conditioners that hadn't run since 1972, and unstable ceilings.

"I think it's going to take a little more than drywall compound to fix this place up," Ray said in a slow drawl.

"No kidding. That's for repairing the apartment where my daughter and I are living." Drew waved at the main house. "As you can see, you're right. A total dump."

Ray said nothing for a long time, then he left the truck and walked to the main house, stopping shy of the porch and gazing up at it, hands at his sides.

Drew joined him. "It doesn't look any better from here."

Ray glanced down at her, his green eyes unreadable. "You really going to reopen it?"

"I don't have a choice." She put her hands on her hips. "I mean, I do, but I don't. My grandfather left it to me, but only if I can fix up the B&B and make it pay within a year. If I don't …" Drew made a slicing motion with the side of her hand. "I get nothing. Not the large amount of money waiting for me after that, no property, and I'd still have to pay all the taxes before it gets gifted to a developer, as per the conditions of the trust. And yes, I quit my job to come out here to maybe give my daughter a better life and live on property that has been in my family for generations. *How hard could it be?* I asked myself. And here I am." She regarded the house in growing anger. "I don't know a damn thing about renovating houses, and I don't have the money to hire someone to do it for me. And I don't know why I'm spilling this to you, a total stranger."

Maybe because he stood in companionable silence, letting her talk without judgment.

"Not a *total* stranger." His voice held mirth. "You did dump drywall compound all over me."

Drew's laugh held an edge of hysteria. "I am so, so sorry."

Ray shrugged, powerful shoulders moving. "I live on a ranch with cows and horses. What do you think *they* dump on me? Not to mention my little brother."

A man with cows and horses and a younger brother sounded more normal and human and real.

Not that Ray Malory was fake in any way. He had a presence that had made the Fullers, father and son, fade into the background. He'd taken over, loaded her stuff, led the way out, and now looked over the house as though he knew exactly what he'd do with it.

"Mom?" The door that led to the stairs to the apartment banged open, and Erica charged out, colt-like limbs flying. "Who's this?"

She didn't ask the question in timidity, fear, or with any caution. Not Erica. Her daughter was a tough kid from the city—at least, that was how she saw herself.

"Ray Malory," Drew said quickly. "From Riverbend. He helped me bring the supplies from the hardware store."

"Oh, sure, you went shopping and came back with a *guy*." Erica grinned. "Hi, I'm Erica," she said to Ray. "You single?"

"*Erica!*" Drew turned to Ray in mortification. "I'm sorry. I found her on my doorstep one day and made the mistake of feeding her."

Erica chortled. "That would be funny if I didn't look just like you."

"It's okay." Ray, fortunately, was amused. "I am single, as it happens. So's my brother. But I think he has a crush on the vet."

"The vet?" Erica widened her eyes. "As in veterinarian? Girl vet or boy vet? Is your brother gay?" She asked in avid curiosity, with no condemnation.

Ray's mouth twitched. "Dr. Anna is a lady. If my brother is gay, he hasn't told me."

"Would be so cool if he was gay."

Ray rubbed his lower lip. "He might be. I'll ask him."

Drew cut off the conversation before it spun out of control. "Erica, did you finish sanding those cupboards?"

"Yep. Smooth as a baby's bottom. Not that I've ever touched one. Gross. Have you been inside our wreck, Ray?" Erica waved at the house. "It's a pile of garbage. And this town is nothings-ville in the middle of nowhere. It doesn't even have a *mall*. I mean, where do you shop?"

Drew quivered in embarrassment. "Apologize, Erica. You don't move into someone's hometown and criticize it. There are malls in Austin. We saw them on the way through, remember?"

"Yeah, but that's so far *away*. Sorry, Ray. I bet you love this place. Riverbend. All five square feet of it."

"I do love it." Ray spoke without defensiveness. "But it takes some getting used to. I grew up here, so I know every-thing about it, good and bad." He looked down at Erica, at his ease. "We don't have malls because they'd go out of business, but we have the best pies on the planet at Mrs. Ward's, and most people in Riverbend have got your back."

Erica listened, actually listened, and even looked thought-ful. "Well, maybe I'll give it some more time. I doubt we'll stay long. Mom won't be able to save this place, and we'll go back home."

She stated this with conviction. Erica hadn't wanted to move to Riverbend, and Drew didn't blame her. Erica had friends, connections, a life back in Chicago. But she'd also had to dodge gang kids and drug dealers right on the school grounds. Not that small towns didn't have drug problems— they did, more than people knew—but Drew had decided she didn't want Erica being threatened anymore.

Before Drew could answer, the peace of the late afternoon was shattered by a long, drawn-out scream.

Drew whipped her head around to stare at the house. Shadows were lengthening, the September day starting to die. The cry came from inside the derelict house, like a shriek from an unholy creature caught in hell.

Chapter Two

The scream sounded again, loud and haunting. As soon as Ray's heartbeat returned to somewhere near normal, he started for the house.

Drew and Erica did as well, but they stayed behind him. Drew looked worried, Erica torn between fear and morbid curiosity.

While most of the county thought the old Paresky place was haunted, Ray didn't believe in ghosts. He *had*, for a split second when they heard the wail, but then realized logically it must be an animal trapped.

He carefully went up the porch steps, putting his weight where he figured the joists that held up the porch floor lay. No way did he want to plunge through rotted boards into whatever was underneath the house.

Drew followed him, admonishing Erica to stay put, and stepping where he did.

The front door came off the hinges when Ray pushed on it. The door had been locked with a dead bolt, but that didn't matter because the bolt tore right out of the wall as the door fell inward.

The howls increased as Ray cautiously stepped inside the house. The front hall ran from front to back, with a staircase missing half its stairs on one side. Doors to the right and left led to rooms, big ones in front, light flooding through the windows.

Ray moved carefully into the room that had once been a living room, and sneezed. Dust coated everything, that special Texas dust that drifted back down as soon as the furniture was wiped. The floor was thick with it, except for a small set of paw prints leading to the fireplace.

Drew was going to have a hell of a time cleaning this place up. Ray wanted to tell her to bulldoze the house to the ground and start again, but he knew she didn't want to hear that.

She was cute too, with brown hair and blue eyes behind dark lashes, a roundish face that scrunched up too much in concern. Ray would love to smooth the worry lines away with his fingers, tell her everything would be all right.

He wasn't sure why he reacted that way to her, but he didn't have the time or inclination to analyze his feelings. Ray wasn't the rescue-the-damsel type, but something about her had made him want to carry her supplies home and now rush in to find out what kind of animal had gotten itself stuck in her house.

Ray reached the fireplace and knelt down. The hearth was as filthy as the rest of the room, but he was already coated with drywall powder, so what the hell?

The cries escalated, whatever it was wanting *out*.

"I think it's up in the chimney." Ray stuck his head inside and found he couldn't see much. "Got a flashlight?"

One tapped him, held by Erica, who obviously hadn't obeyed her mom. Drew said nothing, only held Erica gently back while Ray flashed the light up into the chimney again.

He saw no animal, only soot-covered brick and the damper, closed. He reached up, finding the chain that held it shut.

"Okay, I'm going to open this. You might want to wait in the hall, in case half the chimney comes down with it."

Drew retreated across the room. Erica, though she gazed longingly at the fireplace as though she'd like to see that disaster, went with her.

Mother and daughter hovered in the doorway, Erica a smaller version of Drew, though Erica had a narrower face and a set of shoulders that likely came from her father.

Who was her dad anyway? And why wasn't *he* here, looking up chimneys and repairing drywall?

Ray turned his face from the fireplace and closed his eyes as he tugged at the chains that held the damper closed. At home, he'd have spread newspaper or plastic all over the floor, but there wasn't much point in this wreck of a living room.

The panel inside the chimney gave. Soot, twigs, bits of brick, and who the hell knew what else tumbled down into the fireplace. Ray held his breath, ducking swiftly away.

The cries only worsened. Whatever had been on top of the damper was still inside, terrified now that its platform was gone.

Ray switched on the flashlight again and looked up. He saw the gleam of eyes and teeth in the saddest and scrawniest looking feline he'd ever seen.

"It's a cat," he announced.

"Oh," Erica crooned. "Oh, poor thing. Can you get it out?"

Ray reached up, but the cat was too far away, clinging with claws to the bricks it was afraid to climb down.

He wasn't certain he could rescue it. But with Drew watching him, and Erica, her lip trembling, Ray couldn't say no. He'd get that cat out, even if he had to tear down the chimney to do so.

Ray calculated that if he stood up straight in the chimney, he might just about reach the cat, if it didn't start crawling up the bricks away from him.

He ducked out of the fireplace. "You got anything I can stand on? The fireplace is huge. A stool or chair will fit."

Drew's eyes had gone wide, but not with fear. She pressed her hand to her mouth, stifling a choke of laughter. Erica was already squealing with it.

"Sorry," Drew said. "But you should see yourself."

Ray gazed down at his soot-streaked and white dusted shirt. He was a mess, and his face must be covered with dirt and muck. "Oh well. I'm not going anywhere fancy."

"Stay right there." Drew steered Erica out, Erica's peals of laughter escalating as they went out the front door.

Ray watched through the broken window as they jogged to the garage, mother and daughter side-by-side, voices fresh and clear.

The house was a wreck, but as Ray glanced around, he could see it had a solidness to it. The interior needed a lot of work, including fumigation and mold blasting, but the structure of the house was sturdily built. They'd made houses to last in the old days. The fireplace and chimney, by the look of them, would probably stand until the end of time.

Drew returned with a stepladder, which Erica helped guide through the door. The cat's howls had quieted a bit, winding down to a pathetic mewling.

Ray slid the ladder into the chimney and began his ascent. He had to hold on to the walls, which meant more soot on his hands. The cat regarded him with deep suspicion.

"It's okay," he said to it in the tone he used on foals, calves, or puppies. "I'm here to help you."

The cat tried to scramble away from him, but gravity started to win. Claws latched into the brick, the cat amazingly strong. When Ray put his hand up, ready to grab the cat by the scruff, one set of claws transferred itself to his wrist. Ray suppressed a yelp and closed the other hand on the cat, but it squirmed out of his grasp.

Ray reached again. All at once, the cat, who either decided Ray was its rescuer or a convenient ladder, dropped onto his head.

Quickly Ray closed his grip around the cat's body, pulling it from him as he stepped back down the ladder.

The cat was a limp ball by the time he ducked out of the fireplace again. Blood trickled down his forehead to sting his eyes and blur his vision.

A pair of cool hands took the cat from him. Ray wiped his face with his sleeve and opened his eyes to see the cat snuggled against Drew's chest. It began to purr.

"Aw," Erica crooned. "What a sweetie. Can we keep it? Mom, say we can keep it."

"Well, I'm not throwing it out to fend for itself." Drew stroked the filthy cat's head with her thumb. "But we should have it checked it out and make sure it's all right."

"By the lady vet?" Erica gently pet the cat with one finger —Ray noted that she was careful not to startle it.

"Sure, Dr. Anna will take a look," Ray said. "Want me to call her?"

"It's no bother," Drew said quickly. "I can make an appointment. Where is the vet clinic?"

"Out the other side of town a ways. But she can drop by on her rounds." Ray slid his phone, which thankfully had remained somewhat clean, out of his pocket. He thumbed through his contacts until he found Anna's number and punched it.

"Dr. Anna!" she sang out, her voice sounding distant. Must be on her car phone.

Ray explained the situation, and Anna said, "No problem. I just finished at the Jones's, so I'm close. See you in a few."

Drew blinked when Anna hung up. "That's nice of her. You sure she doesn't mind?"

Ray grinned. "Dr. Anna loves animals better than people. She's happy to help out an animal in need, large or small."

"I want to be a vet," Erica declared.

"Yesterday you wanted to be a horseback rider," Drew countered, as though this was an ongoing discussion.

"I can be both. Horses need vets. Ray, I want to have ten horses, and their names will be …"

"It can wait," Drew said hastily. She transferred her gaze to Ray. "You look horrible. Come inside and wash up." She cuddled the cat closer. "And I bet this one would like a can of tuna."

Ray suppressed a grin as he nodded. He'd get himself stuck in a fireplace and covered with soot and drywall powder more often if it made a pretty woman ask him over.

AFTER RAY SET THE BROKEN FRONT DOOR BACK IN ITS opening, Drew led them all across the drive to the garage.

Ray was truly filthy, his face coated in black and white, like bizarre clown makeup.

He'd gone above and beyond crawling up the chimney after a stray cat, which was almost as grimy as Ray.

Erica was already taken with the cat. She'd always wanted a pet, but living in a small apartment in a building that didn't take pets, and before that with a man who didn't like animals, she'd never had a chance. Drew had seen moving to Riverbend as a chance to give Erica pets, friends, a town she wasn't afraid to walk in.

Drew hadn't planned on a pet so quickly, but the cat, a young one by the look of it, settled against Drew and announced it wasn't leaving.

Erica skipped ahead, eagerly opening the door to admit Ray. She led the way upstairs to the garage apartment, which had a living room with tiny kitchen in front, a large bedroom and a smaller one in back, and a decent-sized bathroom.

Grandfather Paresky's furniture, which was about forty years old, filled the apartment, from his sagging bed to his old lounge chair which he'd obviously loved. Drew had brought her own sheets and towels with her to replace the threadbare ones, but she'd left most of her things in storage, as the lawyer who'd communicated with her about the B&B had said it was furnished. He just hadn't said "furnished with things about to fall apart."

Ray glanced around with the same assessing look he'd given the main house. His gaze went to the holes in the drywall, the single-paned windows that creaked in the slight breeze, the water stains on the ceiling.

"Bathroom's through here," Drew said. "Hot water works at least."

She doubted washing off in the sink would help Ray

much. He needed to strip down and take a full shower. The idea of a man as good looking as Ray naked in her shower—even with the door closed and locked behind him—made a new fire begin in her belly, one she hadn't felt in a long, long time.

"It's okay," Ray said in his slow drawl. Drew already loved the Texas accent, something her grandmother had slaked long ago. "I'll rinse off with your spigot outside and be on my way."

He must have seen something in her eyes, a reluctance to let him linger. Her reluctance had to do with her own history and pain, not him. He'd been so nice, and now he offered to clear out when he was a mess because of her.

Drew impulsively put a hand on his arm. She instantly snatched it away, the strength she'd felt under his skin making her shake. "It's no bother. You go in there and use real soap and water. I'll grab you some clean towels."

"They won't be clean for long," Ray warned. His green eyes twinkled from the soot and powder coating his face.

"It's okay," Erica said around Drew. "They're old. We never get anything new."

"Get the towels out of the box, Erica," Drew said firmly. "Ray, you wash up, and I'll feed the cat."

She turned away before she could stare at Ray any longer, and marched into the kitchen. She and Erica had plenty of canned food to eat, because she'd stocked up at a supermarket in Austin, not knowing what grocery stores, if any, she'd find in Riverbend. She'd since learned that there was a nice, locally owned grocery near the diner, though she'd been subject to many curious gazes the sole time she'd entered it.

The cat tried to climb Drew's leg as soon as she set it

down, small claws piercing her jeans. Drew took out a can of tuna with a pull-off top and opened it. She found a glass bowl and dumped the contents into it, not wanting the cat to cut itself on the can.

The cat ceased trying to climb her once the bowl was on the floor. It dove in, jaws working to eat the tuna, devouring half of it in about ten seconds.

Drew heard Erica's laughter and then running water, and ducked back through the Drew's bedroom to the bathroom.

Ray, sleeves rolled up, splashed in the sink, the water and the sink's bowl already dirty. Erica stood in the doorway, chattering nonstop, her arms full of every clean towel they'd brought from Chicago.

"... And my friend Rachel, she bets I'll never ride horses, but I can, right? I just need to find a horse."

Drew waited for Ray to growl at her to go away, or ignore her completely, but Ray sluiced water over his face and answered, "My sister's stepdaughter gives riding lessons. She could teach you. Her name's Faith."

"*Sweet.* Can I meet her?"

"Erica, let him dry himself off before you bombard him with questions," Drew said in exasperation.

Erica gave her mom an impatient look, but she closed her mouth. Made a show of it, pressing her lips together.

Ray grabbed the top towel from Erica's pile. "I don't mind. I'll ask Faith. Bet she'd love to show you how to ride. She's about the same age as Erica," he told Drew.

For the first time since Erica had learned she had to leave everything she'd ever known and relocate to Texas, she looked excited. Ray kept doing Drew favors.

He toweled off his face then looked at the cloth, which came away gray. "Sorry about that."

"It'll wash," Drew said quickly. "That is, if we had a washing machine that worked."

"There's a washer and dryer in the garage downstairs," Erica said. "But they're old. Probably haven't been run in ages. Great-grandpa must never have washed his clothes."

"He had a housekeeper," Ray said. He continued to dry his hands, smearing the towel more, but not his fault. "Kept the place up the best she could and took his laundry home with her to do."

"Is she dead too?" Erica asked.

Ray chuckled, a warm rumble. "No, she lives in town and works for Mrs. Ward now. Mrs. Ward owns the diner."

"We have diners in Chicago. I never go there." Erica wrinkled her nose. She preferred fast food with her friends, though Drew had already explained Riverbend didn't have her favorite chains.

"You'd like Mrs. Ward's. I already told you about her pie."

Erica looked marginally interested. "Well, maybe we could try the pie."

"Sure." Ray turned to Drew as he continued to wipe his hands. "Maybe you two would come with me one night. I'm kind of a mess right now …"

Drew met his green eyes for a brief moment before she flushed and looked away. Was he asking her out?

No, just being nice. He'd included Erica. Had it been so long since she'd gone on a date that she couldn't tell if a man was asking her out?

Yes.

She wet her lips, but before she could answer, the sound of a truck pulling in outside interrupted them. Drew hurried to the front window and saw a pickup with a small trailer park behind Ray's truck.

A small young woman emerged from the driver's side of the tall truck, sliding a long way down before she landed on her feet. She wore jeans, boots, and a polo top, her blond hair in a neat braid coiled around her head. She took a bag from the truck and then scanned the garage, probably looking for signs of life.

Drew waved at her out the window then returned to the kitchen to scoop up the cat, who was licking the long-empty bowl of tuna. Savoring every drop.

She carried the cat down the stairs with her and opened the door at the bottom just as the young woman poised her hand to knock.

"Hello," the woman said in a pleasant voice. "I'm Dr. Anna. This is the patient?"

Chapter Three

❧❦❧

Damn. Ray finished drying his hands and face, embarrassed at the amount of dirt that transferred to the towel.

Dr. Anna had arrived too quickly—Drew'd turned abruptly away before she could answer Ray's question, as though relieved she didn't have to.

Erica abandoned Ray instantly to run down the stairs after her mother. She was cute, and restless in a pre-teen way. Be good for her and Faith to meet.

Her mom, now. Ray scrunched the towel as he thought about Drew's dark hair in unruly waves, blue eyes like a twilight sky. Nice body too, plenty of curves under her shapeless top and baggy jeans. Drew had put on those clothes to work, but Ray couldn't help picturing her in a form-hugging dress or slim pants, showing off all she had.

His invitation to the diner hadn't come out right, and he'd included Erica, in case Drew got the wrong idea.

Or rather, the *right* idea. Ray wanted to take this woman out, get to know her, find out what she was like under the sloppy work clothes. *Who* she was, what had happened in her previous life, was she still single, and would she be interested in a cowboy like Ray?

Dr. Anna's arrival had cut off her answer. Hell.

Ray started to discard the towel in the bathroom's hamper but balked. He couldn't leave this disgusting thing for Drew to take care of. He'd take it home and wash it for her.

He tucked the towel under his arm and went downstairs and out the door to where the three women were cooing over the cat.

Anna tickled it under the chin, making friends as she did with all animals. "It's a little girl cat," she told Erica. "What's her name?"

"We don't know yet," Drew began.

Erica broke in. "What about Cinders? Like Cinderella? Because we found her in the fireplace."

Drew smiled, her beauty shining out. "A great idea."

"I'll check her over, but I'll say right now you'll have to bathe her in flea shampoo," Anna said. "I'll give her some worm medicine too, in case. She's obviously been on her own a while."

"Poor Cinders." Erica stroked the cat's head. It closed its eyes, purring under the attention. "We'll take care of you from now on."

Erica had a good heart. Meant her mom had taught her compassion, a trait mostly learned by example.

Drew saw Ray and turned that smile on him, making Ray all kinds of warm. "Ray rescued her. Climbed right up the chimney and pulled her out."

"I can tell." Dr. Anna's gaze took in the mess of Ray's clothes and his face blotched with the soot he hadn't been able to rub off. She turned to the cat, and Ray saw her flush rise. "So how's Kyle doing?" she asked, as though offhand.

Ray suppressed a grin. "Not too bad. He's on pain meds and can't move around much, which makes him seriously cranky. Hard to live with. I'll be glad when he's better, for both our sakes. He had a bad fall off a bull," Ray added for Drew and Erica.

"Oh, I'm sorry," Drew said at once. "Is he all right?"

"Busted a couple ribs, pulled a lot of muscles." Ray shrugged. "He's been hurt a lot worse. Like I said, he's healing. And cranky."

"Bull riding is dangerous," Dr. Anna said with a growl. "I don't understand why he does it."

Ray noticed she wasn't asking why *Ray* did it. "For the thrill," he answered. "The challenge of riding the wildest bull and proving you can do it. The prize money doesn't hurt."

"Well, it's crazy." Anna took an instrument that looked like a tiny flashlight from her pocket and examined the cat's ears and eyes.

"I'll tell him you said hi," Ray said, with a wink at Drew and Erica. Kyle would snarl and not believe him, but it was entertaining to tease his little brother.

Anna went a darker shade of red, her attention firmly on the cat. "I hope he gets better soon."

"We all do." Ray nodded at Drew. "I'm going to offload the rest of your stuff and go. Need to clean up."

He gave the collected ladies another nod—they were all looking at him now—and made himself walk away.

He heard footsteps behind him. "Ray. Um ..."

Ray turned. Beyond Drew, Dr. Anna said, "Erica, will you help me check out Cinders? I need a table to set her on."

Erica immediately dashed into the garage, and Anna followed.

Drew remained, her lovely eyes fixed on Ray. "Thank you for helping today. Really."

The Ray Malory he knew would say something smooth, like it was a pleasure to help out a pretty woman, but his tongue stuck to the roof of his mouth. He hadn't helped her simply because she was gorgeous, or even pitiable. He'd felt a pull to her that unnerved him.

"It's no trouble." The words came out awkwardly, and Ray cleared his throat. "If you want, I can come tomorrow, help you start sorting things out. This is going to be a big job."

Her smile vanished. Hell, now she probably thought he was angling for her to pay him.

"I don't know …" she began.

Ray raised his hands. "I mean as a friend. Helping out. That house is a wreck. I hate for you to dig through it by yourself."

"I did plan to hire someone to help. The Fullers have a guy, they said."

Ray was already shaking his head. "Nah, he'd rather sit on his butt all day than work. He's Fuller's cousin, and they owe his mom a favor, so they can't fire him."

"Oh."

"How about we talk about it tomorrow? I can tell you who's good and who isn't."

Drew's smile returned. "I'd appreciate it. I admit I have no idea what I've gotten myself into."

"See you tomorrow then." Ray tried to sound casual, pretend something in him wasn't dancing in glee at the prospect of hanging out with her again.

"Thanks, Ray."

He liked the way she said his name. No different from the way anyone else did, he supposed, but for some reason it sounded better from her lips.

Ray forced himself to walk away. Not easy with the sunshine on Drew's hair, her smile making her eyes dance. But he'd be back. He'd be back as often as he could.

THE MALORY RANCH WAS HUMMING ALONG AS USUAL WHEN Ray reached it. Their small herd dotted the far hill, the cattle enjoying the fair weather. A trainer worked a cutting horse in the ring, its owner observing from the rail.

Ray gave the trainer and owner a nod and headed to the house, stripping down once he slammed the back door. One advantage of all the females having moved out was that Ray could take off his clothes in the kitchen and stuff them into the washing machine in the tiny laundry room behind it.

In his underwear, Ray added Drew's towel and soap, adjusted settings, and pushed start. His mom and sisters had taught both brothers how to run the machine a long time ago, saying they weren't about to be Ray's and Kyle's laundrywomen.

Kyle's voice sounded behind him. "Oh, hell, this is all I need."

Ray turned to regard his brother, his tanned face wan with pain, leaning heavily on a walking stick in the middle of the kitchen.

"I finally convince myself to come downstairs, and I see *that.*" Kyle made a face at Ray's mostly naked and grime-streaked body. "What happened to you?"

Ray knew Kyle would hear about his adventure from

Craig at the feed store, and maybe Anna, if she felt like talking to him. But for some reason, Ray didn't want to tell his brother about Drew's soft smile or the sparkle in her eyes. Kyle would rag him, as he always did when Ray so much as looked at a woman with interest.

To be fair, Ray did the same thing to Kyle, but a reluctance to discuss Drew came over him. Until he explored this tentative thing he felt about the woman he'd met today—if it was a thing at all—it was Ray's business and no one else's.

"Some shit fell on me at the feed store," he extemporized. "Not actual shit—drywall compound and stuff."

"Well, wash it off. I hear that stuff's not good to breathe in."

"Why do you think I'm standing here in my underwear? I'm heading for the shower. How you doing?"

"I'm in pain. Fucked up from meds. Bored. How do you think I'm doing?"

"Well, you can always help Margaret in the office. Sweet talk people on the phone or something."

Kyle's gaze went to the window and the horse and rider in the ring beyond. "Yeah, that sounds like fun."

"Better than moping around on your ass," Ray said, not unkindly. "You'll heal, bro. It just takes time."

"I know that." Kyle moved restlessly. "This wasn't my first rodeo." He quirked his lips at his feeble joke. "Yeah, think I'll hobble down and see if Margaret needs anything. Wish me luck."

He meant with Margaret, their formidable office manager, not the walk to the trailer at the end of the drive.

"You got it. Take it easy."

"Whatever." Kyle growled and stumped out the door.

Ray shook his head and trudged upstairs, stripped off his

boxer briefs, and stepped into the shower. The water and soap erased the layers of soot and dried blood that caked his skin, but when Ray closed his eyes to rinse off, all he could think of was Drew's big smile when she'd watched Ray climb out of the fireplace with the cat, and laughed at him.

***

"MOM! RAY'S HERE!"

Erica bounced up the stairs, the cat running on wiry legs behind her.

Drew made herself calmly finish stacking the dishes in the draining tray, pretending Erica's announcement barely affected her. She reflected that she missed having a dishwasher, but at least Erica was good about helping wash them without complaint.

Drew tried not to hurry to the living room window once she was done. *Walk slowly, no big deal.* The last few steps were too quick for her comfort, and she peered eagerly down.

Below them, Ray slid out of his big, gleaming pickup, black cowboy hat firmly on his head. He wore a loose brown T-shirt with a canted black letter M emblazoned on it. Jeans hugged his very nice butt, and dusty cowboy boots completed the picture.

Guys who'd worn cowboy attire at Drew's high school had been dismissively called "drugstore" cowboys, meaning they'd probably never been on a horse or seen a cow in their lives. Ray was the real thing. Drew had come to Texas with the vague idea that working cowboys were rail thin, always dusty, and spit a lot. She never dreamed she'd be attracted to one. Ray, with his solid body, square face, and green eyes, was changing her mind.

He spied her in the window and raised a hand in greeting.

Drew waved back, left the window, and started down the stairs to the garage. She caught herself smoothing her hair, and forced her hands to her sides. He was here being nice, that was all.

Erica had charged down the stairs ahead of her and ran for the pickup. "Morning, Ray! We already had breakfast, or I'd offer you some."

"That's okay. I ate. How's the cat doing?" Ray looked pointedly at the feline who was at Erica's heels.

The cat, once bathed, dried, and brushed, turned out to be a soft grey with very white paws and chest. She had startlingly blue eyes and an impish look as she bounded sideways in her enthusiasm.

"Cinders? She's great. Ate another whole can of tuna. We'll have to get her some cat food."

Erica continued about everything the cat had done since Ray had seen it last, all of eighteen hours ago.

"Erica, don't wear him out," Drew said as she reached them. "She's used up all her talk on me and looking to expand," she said to Ray. "Just tell her to zip it."

Ray shrugged in his good-natured way. "I don't mind. I have sisters. I'm used to it."

"Sisters?" Erica pounced on the information like Cinders had pounced on a roach last night. "What are their names?"

"One is Lucy—she lives in Houston now. The other is Grace. She got married and lives right here in Riverbend. Her stepdaughter is the one I said could give you riding lessons."

"Yes!" Erica danced around, her twelve-year-old energy unrestrained. "Can I, Mom? Oh, please, please, please, please."

"When we're more settled," Drew said. If they *could* be more settled. "Right now, we have a lot of work to do."

Erica took that as affirmation, and ran off, jumping, doing cartwheels, laughing. The cat leapt with her, recognizing a kindred spirit.

That left Drew and Ray facing each other in awkward silence. At least, Drew felt awkward.

"Actually," Ray said, "I brought you some stuff from my sister's bakery."

"Your sister has a bakery?" Drew blurted as he turned back to his truck.

"Grace, yeah." He emerged with a pink box. "She opened a place not long ago. She's an amazing cook."

"Well, we always welcome food." Drew accepted the box, determined not to look inside. From the scent of baked things and chocolate wafting to her, she might start nervously shoveling it in. "At least Erica does. She can put it away and instantly run it off. Young adrenaline."

"Yep, I was like that as a kid. Lanky and always moving."

He'd filled out since then, obviously. Ray had a solid body, muscles stretching even his loose shirt.

Drew could stand and stare at his muscles all day, or she could make use of his niceness and get some work done. She hurriedly carried the box upstairs and left it on the counter —making certain it was securely closed against inquisitive cat paws—and clattered downstairs again.

She joined Ray who studied the house while leaning against his pickup. "I'm not sure where to start," Drew said. "Tear it down and build again?"

"Nah, I don't think you have to. When I was stuck up your chimney, I noticed it was a pretty solid house. Take the rotted stuff out, redo plumbing and wiring, reshingle the roof, and you should be fine." Ray slanted her a grin. "That's all."

"When you put it like that ..." Drew covered her face. "I should give up now and go home."

"I think it's doable." He sounded confident. "It will take time and money, is all. Let's have a look."

Time and money. Sure. Like either of those hung in the air, waiting for Drew to reach for them.

"How do we look without getting hurt?" Drew eyed the sagging porch and the door Ray had propped up in the opening as they'd exited yesterday. "It's not exactly stable in there."

"Very carefully. But I think Erica should stay out for a while."

"Ha. Good luck with that."

"At least she's fearless. That can be a good thing—you know, if she doesn't hurt herself. As for us, I brought these ..."

He trailed off and rummaged in the bed of his truck, emerging with two hard hats. He handed her one.

Drew took it in wonder. "Are you a construction worker?" She should be so lucky.

"No, I had these for spelunking. I have lights too, if we need them."

Drew adjusted the straps inside the hat and put it on. "You do spelunking in Texas? I thought it was mostly flat."

"There's plenty of caves in the Hill Country—where there's limestone and water, you get caves. Some can be seen on tours, but others are out there for true exploring. I haven't gone in a while, but I've kept the gear."

Ray was full of surprises, and wasn't the stereotype she'd imagined. Riverbend wasn't what she'd imagined either—

she'd thought it would be a dusty town in the middle of nowhere with no trees, its inhabitants on horseback or in old broken-down cars.

Instead Drew had found sweeping green hills, stands of live oak and swaths of flowers, cars of the latest models, and horses and cows meandering in pastures. Now she'd just learned there were caves to explore.

Ray was far more polite than any man she'd ever met, and also courteous, nice to her daughter, and compassionate enough to rescue a cat from a chimney. In short, a kind human being.

She wasn't sure what to do with that.

"I guess I'm ready," she said. "Let me find out what I'm facing."

Ray exchanged his cowboy hat for a hardhat, grabbed a flashlight, and led the way to the house. Drew caught herself watching him walk, the movement of his very tight backside distracting.

He stepped up on the porch, taking his time to shine the flashlight on the ceiling there. He didn't have to point out all the cracks—Drew saw them just fine.

The porch posts were rotting as well. It was too bad, because they were beautiful, pleasingly carved and laced with gingerbread at the top. Drew wondered if any could be saved.

Ray set aside the broken door, carefully stepping where they'd walked the day before. Three sets of human footprints and one of cat lay in the thick dust, a reminder of yesterday's dramatic rescue.

Ray flashed his light into corners, at door frames, and at the ceiling as they walked, head tilted to examine what he lit up.

"Any hope?" Drew asked as they entered what had been the dining room.

"Maybe." Ray's tone was cautious, as though he didn't want to commit himself. "You might have to—"

His words cut off as a ceiling beam chose that moment to fall down at him, a huge chunk of plaster and board coming with it.

Chapter Four

As Ray dove aside, he heard another tearing sound, and
Drew shrieked. He threw off the debris trying to bury
him and ran at her, shoving her back into the hall as a second
beam came down.

They landed against the wall by the doorway, dust
coating the air. Ray held his breath and Drew coughed.

She was soft beneath him, eyes round in shock. Her hard
hat had canted to the side of her head, which for some
reason was sexy as hell.

"I'm so sorry." Drew coughed some more. "This place is a
death trap."

Ray should tell her not to worry, that this was why he'd
brought the hats, but he couldn't speak.

She was tight against him, her cheeks streaked with dust,
dark curls sticking to her forehead. Drew's concern was for
him, no matter that he'd pushed her out of the way of the
upstairs trying to come downstairs.

Ray touched her cheek with a blunt finger. Her gaze

flicked up to him, catching him like sunlight on glass, the glow of her almost cutting.

He watched himself as though from far way drawing closer and closer, the space between them heating as their bodies neared. When Ray was a breath away, he ceased trying halt himself.

Her lips were parted, red, warm. He kissed them.

Drew startled gasp touched his mouth, then she lifted herself to meet the kiss.

Her mouth was strong but supple, seeking and tender at the same time. She launched her body against his, hands on his shoulders as though trying to steady them both.

Ray gentled her with a hand on her back, pulling her closer to kiss her deeply, opening her mouth with his.

She tasted of coffee, sweetness, and worry. Beautiful lady. She kissed like fire, but kept pulling back a little, then kissing harder, as though she couldn't decide which to do.

Ray ran his hand to the back of her neck, under her hair, scooping her closer. His tongue tangled with hers, his heart easing as he drank her in.

Her mouth was a place of tenderness, body flowing to him as though she belonged there. Ray held her in place, his need rising, wanting him to teach her that she did belong against him, no matter what.

Drew jerked, as though realizing what she was doing. Her head went back, her mouth breaking from his.

She gazed up at him with heat in her eyes, but also uncertainty. He read hurt deep inside her, and the fear it would happen again.

As they looked at each other, silence hanging like the dust, Drew blushed a deep red.

"I am so sorry," she said in a near-whisper.

Ray's mouth stretched in a grin. "Why? I'm not."

"I don't usually ..."

"Kiss a person you just met?" Ray rested his arm above her on the wall. "Neither do I, but I thought I'd make an exception."

"Because we were almost killed?"

"Partly." Ray leaned a little closer. "And partly because you're a pretty woman. And a nice one."

"Not really."

"Huh. Bet me." Ray touched her face, liking how it flushed even more. "You're sweet, and you're alone. Don't let cowboys take advantage of you."

"I'm not." A sparkle entered Drew's eyes. "I'm using you shamelessly to help me with this wreck of a house. And I kissed *you*."

"We can debate that. Seems like it was mostly mutual kissing."

She took a breath, as though she wanted to argue, then she sent him a faint smile. "Yeah, it was."

"Maybe sometime we can do it again." Ray kept his voice casual, but his heart thumped wildly in anticipation. Damn, but he wanted to do it again. "You know, when we're not afraid of a house falling on us."

She smiled back, but Ray could tell she wasn't mentally marking a time in her datebook to kiss him again. Oh well.

Didn't mean Ray would simply give up. He hadn't gone out much since his spectacular breakup with Christina Campbell, and he saw in Drew the same reticence to trust, to care, as he felt in himself. At the same time, he sensed her hunger—the need to be in someone's arms, to be held and treasured. And hell, need for the mindless pleasure of sex.

Maybe they could work something out ...

"Come on," he forced himself to say. "Let's get out of here before more beams drop on us."

Drew nodded. She leaned to pick up her hard hat, which had fallen to the floor during their impromptu kiss. She was close to Ray when she rose, and he noticed she gave his body a once-over all the way up.

Yeah, there could be something here, he thought, his body on fire just from her looking at it. Ray wouldn't give up until he knew for sure what.

DREW WALKED BACK TO THE GARAGE NEXT TO RAY, HER BODY flushing then chilling as emotion after emotion rushed through her.

The kiss had been ... amazing. Her lips tingled, her blood burned. She hadn't kissed a man in she couldn't remember how long. She hadn't dated hardly at all since she'd dredged up the courage to kick out Erica's father, and anything since then had been extremely casual.

What she'd felt when Ray had enclosed her in his body and kissed her in that slow, sensual way had been anything but casual. A heat she'd forced to stay damped woke up and demanded attention.

Drew shot another glance at his large body, seriously good-looking face, eyes of deep jade. What woman wouldn't melt when he touched her?

Probably a lot of them did. He was a rodeo cowboy, a bull rider, a man who put himself in danger for the fun of it. He must have plenty of women chasing after him.

Not that she'd noticed any at the hardware store or following him to the B&B to see what he was doing. Ray looked a little lonely—though that might be Drew's wishful thinking.

Ray left her side to unload more things from his truck. He'd brought tools and a ladder, things she hadn't purchased yesterday. He carried these upstairs to start patching the holes in the drywall and announced she should paint the entire interior. He could help.

He'd be coming back, Drew thought with warmth as he spoke matter-of-factly. She really wished she didn't feel so glad.

RAY CAME OVER EVERY DAY FOR THE NEXT WEEK. THEY FELL into a rhythm, Drew fixing an extra portion of breakfast and double the coffee. Ray would show up around nine and knock politely at the door downstairs, which Erica would run and open for him. By the middle of the week, Erica simply dashed down the stairs whenever she saw Ray's truck pull in.

Ray would insist Drew didn't need to feed him, then he'd say, "Well, maybe a little bit," and enjoy eggs and bacon, potatoes and toast. Pancakes one day.

He'd thank her and help clean up the dishes. Then he'd move to whatever they were working on and start in.

Drew worked right alongside him, smearing on drywall joint compound, taping and priming each room after they dragged out the furniture, and then helping rip up the threadbare carpet to reveal beautiful, old hardwood beneath.

"I could make these rooms a suite," Drew said, gazing at the glow of the wood, which Ray said was golden oak. "For honeymoon couples maybe, or people who want to splurge on a romantic weekend."

"Now you're thinking like a business owner." Ray nodded at her. "It's a good idea. Decorate it up, make it a special hideaway. My sister Grace is good at the frilly stuff. She'd be happy to help." He glanced at Drew as he rubbed his sweaty face on the short sleeve of his T-shirt. "She wouldn't take over or anything," he added quickly. "Just give you advice."

"Which I'd take. I have no idea what I'm doing." Drew left the floor to plunk herself on the drop cloth-draped sofa. "You call me business owner, but this is all new territory to me."

Ray rose and went to the kitchen, opening the refrigerator. "What did you do in Chicago?"

Drew hesitated, studying the patch of flooring they'd uncovered. A plastic bottle studded with beads of condensation moved into her view, and she took it gratefully.

"I was a librarian." The words came out a bit defensively.

"No shit?" Ray looked around for a place to sit, but at the moment there was nowhere except the sofa Drew already occupied—they'd moved the rest of the furniture into the bedrooms. She scooted over a little, indicating she didn't mind him next to her.

Which she didn't. The cushions sagged under Ray's warm strength, making Drew want to slide into him.

"Must be a huge library in Chicago," Ray said, sounding admiring.

"I didn't work at the big one downtown. I was in a smaller branch. But it wasn't bad—I had benefits, and Erica could come after school and ride home with me. It's far harder than you'd think to find a decent job as a librarian, even after years of library school ..." Drew groaned as the weight of her decisions struck her. "A good job I quit to come *here.*"

Ray's large hand rested on her back, soothing. "Had to be a tough choice to make."

"It was. And this place is such a mess—I didn't realize how much of a mess. I thought if I could run it or sell it after I opened it— the trust will give me a nice chunk of change if I fix it up and make a go of it. But, it's impossible. Why couldn't my grandfather give me the money *now* so I could use it to fix up the house? If he wanted the B&B running again so much?"

Ray sat in silence, and she didn't really expect him to have an answer. His large hand was comforting though.

The occasional *clank* sounded from the garage below— Erica was cleaning junk from cabinets there, Cinders helping.

Ray cleared his throat. "I asked around about Old Man Paresky—I mean, your grandfather. Seems he was known for being quirky. He loved this place, but after your grand-mother left him, he let it go to ruin. I'd guess he wanted to find out how dedicated you'd be, instead of just giving you the money."

"Because I might find a way to keep the cash without using it to fix up the B&B. I get that." Drew sighed. "Anyone looking at that house would know it was the sensible thing to do."

Ray moved his hand away, and she was suddenly cold. "A nice chunk of change is worth working hard for."

"Compared to the pittance I made, even in a decent library job ... Yeah, I wasn't about to throw that away. I could have signed a paper to give up the trust, let a developer take over, and moved on, but I thought ..." Drew shook her head. "I thought I could do this."

"You still can. You're already getting into the spirit. You had a good idea about making this place a special suite, remember?"

"But I don't know *anything* about running a business." Drew's despair inched back into her. "I've always worked for someone else."

"Well, I do. I've more or less been running a business since I was fourteen."

"Have you?" Drew glanced at him with interest, a big, handsome man who never seemed to hurry, or worry.

"Sure. Cowboys don't just sit around and drink beer, and maybe occasionally get on a horse. A ranch is definitely a business. Kyle and I took over when my dad passed about fifteen years ago. My mom ran it with us for a while, but her heart wasn't in it. She missed my dad too much. She moved to Austin some time ago with Miles—her boyfriend—and left the whole place to me and Kyle. Miles is a good guy, but he's a city man. Ranching's not his thing."

Drew's curiosity stirred as she listened, moroseness fading. "What *do* real cowboys do? I've always wondered."

Ray took a long gulp of water, droplets lingering on his lips. "Kyle and I train horses, we run a small herd of cattle, and we employ a bunch of people to help with all the animals. The prize money Kyle and I make riding in the rodeos we mostly put into the ranch. Training takes a lot of time, and so does the office work. Fortunately, we have Margaret to help out. She's scary, but damn good at her job." He gave her a faint grin. "So, what do real librarians do?"

"More than sit shyly in a corner reading books," Drew answered. "I'm part tour guide, part teacher, part wrangler, part counsellor, part cataloger, part computer geek, part cop. Libraries have become information centers, community centers, makeshift child-care centers, makeshift homeless shelters. Occasionally, we still direct people to the right books. They haven't quite gotten rid of actual books, no matter how far we are into the digital age. Thank heaven. There's something timeless about a book."

"You like to read?"

"I do, actually. I read everything I can." She had to laugh. "I've just gone on about the eternal joy of print, but I love my e-books too. I had to give a lot of my paperbacks away or put them in storage to come out here, so now I read on my phone."

"Lots of books at our ranch," Ray said. "My mom's a big reader, and so is Grace. You could always do a library in your B&B."

Drew felt a surge of renewed eagerness. "I could. I'm imagining people coming out here to get away from it all, to sit on the porch and look at the beautiful scenery, read books, and sip tea."

"Or go hiking, horseback riding, spelunking, boating … lots to do in the Hill Country."

Drew deflated. "I have no idea how to hook people up with what they want to do. Why do I think anyone will come way out here, anyway? Especially when they know what this place looks like?"

She heard her voice take on a note of despair once more. Ray fell silent, but when she turned to him, she saw sympathy in his eyes, not discouragement.

The sight made her sit still. Not since before her marriage thirteen years ago had a man gazed at her in quiet contemplation, neither condemning nor demanding. Philip had been either all over her in passion or deriding her for her family, her cooking, her career choice, and any decision she made about Erica.

Ray simply looked at her in understanding. True, he was a neutral party, a kind person who'd helped her out hauling supplies and who knew about drywalling.

A really good-looking nice guy who knew about drywalling. And didn't stare at her like she'd lost her mind, which was what she'd been getting from her friends and coworkers before she packed up her car and headed south.

The day Ray had rescued the cat, when he'd come out of the bathroom, his hair spiked with his impromptu sponge bath, his skin damp, he'd been delectable. The temptation to kiss him had been high, as it had been in the house when the ceiling had come down and he'd saved her from peril.

As it was now, while he looked at her with water droplets on his lips and understanding in his eyes.

Drew leaned toward him, his body heat drawing her in. Ray remained motionless, watching her come.

"Mom!" Erica's breathless voice cut through the quiet, followed by her running footsteps. She burst in, waving something paperlike. Cinders rushed in after her, jumped to the kitchen counter, and scattered a pile of bolts with a metallic clatter.

"Look what I found." Erica thrust a handful of photographs at Drew, glossy black and whites from long ago. "It's our house. It was beautiful!"

Chapter Five

Ray squeezed his hands around the water bottle, fighting disappointment. Had Drew really started to flow into him, like she wanted to get closer? Or was it just his ego talking?

It didn't matter, because she'd wrenched herself away and now perched on the edge of the sofa, gazing at what Erica had found. Her cheeks were rose-colored, her dark eyes sparkling. A pretty woman, and a sweet one. A lady worth knowing.

A lady with a lot on her mind and on her plate. Ray needed to give her some space, as hard as that was to acknowledge.

"Wow," Drew said. "Look at this place."

She moved the photos so Ray could see them. The pictures were of the B&B about fifty or so years ago, painted and spruced up, the windows whole, the black shingles solid, the brick chimney Ray had spent time inside sturdy. The porch sported lacy curlicues around the pillars.

A 1960s sedan rested in the drive—a long, low, wide car

that, at the time, had meant prosperity. Other shots showed the house from the back, along with a garden in full bloom.

"It *was* beautiful," Drew said admiringly. "I think those are my grandparents."

She pointed to a photo of a couple standing on the front porch, hands on the railing, looking out. They were young, the man black-haired, the woman with her long hair in a ponytail. They stood apart, with some space between them, but they looked contented enough as they gazed at the photographer.

"Must have been right before they split up," Drew said. "My grandmother took my dad to Chicago and never came back to Riverbend."

She sounded sad. It *was* sad when families broke apart, Ray well knew. His dad was gone, his mom in Austin with Miles. Ray and Kyle and their sisters were drifting off now, each in pursuit of their own lives.

"Shows you what you can do with the house, though," Ray offered, shoving aside melancholy thoughts.

"Yes." Drew touched the photo wistfully. "With about a million dollars."

She had a point. Gave Ray an idea, but he'd have to follow up before he blurted it out. Didn't want Drew getting her hopes up for nothing.

Sunlight touched them through the windows, the afternoon waning. Ray glanced at his watch and grimaced.

"I have to go," he said with great reluctance. "My brother, the dumbas—uh, dumb butt—bet Dr. Anna she couldn't ride the mechanical bull at a cowboy bar tonight. I have to drive him—he's still not cleared to drive himself." Ray took in Erica's sudden interest and Drew's blue eyes, and inspiration seized him. "Come with us." He ignored how fast his heart raced as he said the words. "Dr. Anna wouldn't mind, I don't think. Kyle's not a bad guy when he's not complaining, and it will be fun to see Anna win his stupid challenge."

Drew's smile blossomed. Damn, she was beautiful when she smiled. Made Ray want reasons for her do it some more.

Drew took a breath, but whether to accept or turn him down, Ray was not to know. Her cell phone rang at the same instant.

The phone lay across the room on the counter that separated living room from kitchen. Erica leapt to it, snatching it up.

"It's Uncle Jules!" she shouted as she answered it. "Hi, Uncle Jules. This is Erica."

Ray watched Drew's expression change from excited interest to alarm to dismay in the space of a moment. Next came anger, and finally, resignation.

"Your brother?" he asked quietly.

"My dad's brother," Erica announced, holding the phone away. "He wants to talk to you, Mom."

"I have to take this," Drew said, rising. Her face had gone wan, anything welcoming in her eyes vanishing, her body taking on a rigidity Ray hadn't seen before. "Sorry, we won't be able to go tonight."

Ray got to his feet with her, his disappointment acute. Drew remained fixed in place, clearly not about to take the phone while Ray was there.

He swallowed and gave Drew a stiff nod. "See you, then. Stay out of trouble, kid," he said to Erica, who grinned.

Erica held out the phone to her mom, the call from her uncle not concerning her like it did Drew. Why not?

Ray would have to figure it out another time. Drew

waited, her face shuttered, not moving toward Erica or indicating she'd see Ray out.

He caught up his hat, which he'd left hanging on a chair,
gave Drew and Erica another nod, and made his exit. Ray
heard no voices behind him as he clumped down the stairs—
Drew was waiting until Ray moved well out of earshot
before she went for the phone.

Outside, he looked back. Erica, at the window, gave him a
hard and zealous wave. Ray lifted his hand in response,
which elicited a big smile.

He packed up his tools that he'd left lying on the back of
his truck, shut the tailgate, and started up. He pulled out
from the B&B as the sun set, but his mind remained on
Drew and the smile that lit her face, his idea for helping
her, and speculation on why the phone call had unsettled
her.

Ray drove around a long time, lost in thought, before he
remembered to head home and pick up Kyle for the night's
event.

"WHO WAS THAT?" JULES BOLAN DEMANDED.

Drew bit back her angry response as she took the phone
and kept her voice calm. Erica liked Jules, her one link to her
father, and Drew wasn't about to destroy that relationship.

"No one," she said quickly to Jules. "A guy helping us fix
up the place."

"You hired him?" Jules' deep voice was much like Philip's,
a fact that always made Drew shiver. "You should have asked
me—I could have a team down there any time you want."

"No." The word came out sharply, and again, Drew

modulated her voice. "No. It's all right. There's plenty of people here who can do the work."

She had no idea whether there were or not, but she did not want Jules coming to Riverbend to take over. The one thing she'd very much wanted to leave behind in Chicago was Jules.

She didn't worry *too* much about Jules charging to Texas, because he owned a freight shipping business that he was sure would fall apart if he ever took a day off. Also, he hated to spend money on anything but said business.

Jules had made it a policy to keep an eye on Erica—she was a blood relation, and he was big on family sticking together. But while he was lavish with advice that sounded more like commands, he was by no means a generous man with cash.

"I'm meeting with my lawyers tomorrow," Jules said. "There has to be a way for you to get the old man's money without the ridiculous stricture about fixing up the property. Your grandfather had to have been insane—that's what I'm going with. Not of sound mind when he put together the trust."

"I already talked to a ton of lawyers," Drew said, holding on to her patience. "My grandfather knew what he was doing, apparently, and so did the trustees."

"These are *my* lawyers," Jules said. "Used to finding every loophole possible. Don't worry, Drew. We'll get you out of this and sitting on a pile of money. You can come back to Chicago and live in a nice house in Park Ridge or someplace like that."

Jules was always suggesting they move west out of the city, never mind noise from O'Hare. Better for Erica, he said. He was possibly right, but commuting through traffic or even by train was tough. They'd lived ten minutes away from her library, five minutes' walk to Erica's school. Drew hadn't had the money to move, not to mention the time, and as usual, Jules offered no help with the practicalities of his suggestions.

"Is that guy a licensed contractor?" Jules asked. "I didn't think they had them out in the boondocks."

"He's fine."

Drew didn't want to talk about Ray. About how she'd wanted to kiss him. How his hand on her back had been so comforting, how him simply being here made everything easier.

When Ray had asked for them to accompany him tonight, her heart had leapt and then crashed down when Jules had called. She hadn't wanted to talk to Jules in front of Ray, and Ray had understood and gone. Opportunity lost.

"Seriously, Drew, you can get railroaded," Jules was saying. "Make him show you his license. What company does he work for? I can look him up."

"He's local, and it doesn't matter."

"Well, you probably won't need him after my lawyers look at the trust. You can leave the middle of nowhere and come home to civilization. Stop wasting time."

Similar words had gone through Drew's head today as she'd looked over the shelves and shelves and boxes and boxes and junk downstairs. *What am I doing? Why am I wasting my time on this?*

Drew glanced at the photo still clutched in her hand—the one of her young grandfather standing tall on the porch, her grandmother so pretty next to him. She thought of Ray telling her she was already thinking like a B&B owner, and her excitement about decorating the garage apartment as a romantic bower.

"It's not a waste of time," she said brusquely to Jules, cutting off his diatribe. "It's my B&B, and I think I'm going to keep it."

Erica, to her surprise, did a fist pump. No more glum complaining that the nearest mall was sixty miles away.

Jules went off. He wasn't a yeller, but he could assume a severely patient tone of voice and explain, in detail, why Drew was wrong.

Drew held the phone away from her ear while he droned on, then she said abruptly, "Uh oh. I think the toilet's backing up. Gotta go!"

She clicked off the phone and met Erica's gaze. Her daughter wore a grin and rolled her eyes. "He likes a good lecture," Erica said. "Nice one, Mom."

She held up her hand for a high five. Drew smacked Erica's palm with hers and then pulled her daughter into a tight hug.

RAY DIDN'T RETURN THE NEXT DAY. DREW DIDN'T LIKE HOW her heart burned when the road to the B&B remained empty, how quiet it was without Ray's rumbling voice or the low growl of his truck.

He had his own life, she told herself. He had his brother to take care of, and he'd gone to the bar last night, probably with all his friends. She tried not to think of how many attractive women might have been there—ones who came without a rundown house attached.

Besides, Drew had practically run him out, rudely, when

Jules had called. Her brother-in-law sent all Drew's rational thought out the window.

Everyone she'd met in Riverbend so far was friendly and polite, including Ray. Very nice, but she couldn't always tell what people were thinking. In her neighborhood back home, there had been no doubt. It was easy in the city to just push through and know everyone understood you were in a hurry, even if they snarled at you.

Ray had a slow politeness, an easy smile, a drawl that said he had all the time in the world for her.

Drew could call him, ask him for help, but whenever she picked up the phone, she'd look at his name on her contacts and put the phone down again. She didn't know how she'd feel if she asked and he brushed her off.

He'd left enough tools and supplies that Drew and Erica could continue cleaning the garage with no trouble. He'd have to show up sooner or later, she reasoned, to ask for his ladder back.

But Drew didn't see Ray all that day, or the next, or the next. By then, she'd given up looking for him.

On the third day after Jules's call, she and Erica took Cinders to Anna Lawler's vet office for the shots that Dr. Anna had recommended.

Anna's assistant greeted them with a cheerful smile and asked how Drew was settling in—Riverbend hospitality again. Drew waited only a few minutes before Dr. Anna's previous patient emerged, a small dog with its owner, an older woman called Mrs. Kaye. Mrs. Kaye stopped in front of Drew and beamed up at her.

"Hello, Miss Paresky. I knew your grandfather."

The simple statement made Drew still. Most people she'd met in Riverbend referred to her grandfather as "Old Man

Paresky," or "that crazy old guy with the B&B," when they didn't think she could hear them.

"You did?" was all Drew could say.

"Oh, yes," Mrs. Kaye said. "Such a handsome young man. We were all surprised when he married Abby. She was ambitious, always saying she'd shake the dust of Riverbend from her feet. And she did. Lonnie—your grandfather—took it hard."

"I remember my grandmother," Drew said, a lump in her throat. "She took me to museums and art galleries, showed me I could read for the pleasure of it, not just as a school assignment."

Drew pictured her grandmother's soft blue eyes as she'd said, "Never let anyone tell you what to read and more importantly, what *not* to read. What you read is your business. And if you find that book of your heart, it's *yours*. Never let anyone take that away by scoffing at it or saying it's bad for you. How do they know? Read to fill your soul."

Drew had taken the advice to heart, and it had been one reason she'd become a librarian—to help others find those books they loved.

Mrs. Kaye leaned closer. "Your grandmother was unique. We knew she wasn't long for the small-town life. Lonnie, on the other hand, adored Riverbend and his family home. He let it go to wrack and ruin, though. A symbol of his broken heart, I always believed."

Drew thought about the sad and rundown house, waiting for someone to love it again. "You could be right. I hope I can cheer it up."

"You can." Mrs. Kaye patted Drew's shoulder then leaned down and picked up her dog, a cute thing of indeterminate breed. "You'll bring life, and love, and laughter back to the

B&B. You're a Paresky, but you have a lot of your grand-mother in you. I can see it." She gave Drew a long gaze then turned and waved at Dr. Anna's assistant behind her desk. "See you, Janette. I'll email you that cookie recipe."

"Thanks, Mrs. Kaye," Janette answered. "You take care, now."

Mrs. Kaye breezed away, the dog's tail wriggling its entire body.

"She discovered email a couple years ago," Janette, a college-age young woman with dark hair, said to Drew. "And she emails everyone in town. I think she and Craig Fuller's grandpa have an online relationship going, but no one can prove it."

Drew laughed, but she'd been warmed by Mrs. Kaye's words, her belief that Drew would succeed. Ray had a similar confidence ...

Drew shut off the thought. She didn't want to think about Ray right now.

"Hey, Drew. Erica." Dr. Anna came out from her exam room, official in her white coat. "Cinders ready for her shots?"

"We didn't tell her," Erica said seriously. "Didn't want to scare her."

"Good thinking." Anna smiled, but distractedly. She looked a bit wild around the eyes, as though trying to keep calm about something.

"Dr. Anna has a date tonight," Janette announced. "With Kyle Malory. She lost a bet."

"We heard about that," Erica supplied as Anna flushed beet red. "Ray told us a little anyway."

Janette went on before Anna could speak. "Yeah, Dr. Anna promised Kyle she'd go out with him if she couldn't stay on the mechanical bull at Dino's. Such a tragedy, having to let a gorgeous Malory take her to a fancy restaurant."

Drew hadn't seen Kyle yet, but if he looked anything like Ray, then Janette was right—no reason to feel sorry for Anna.

"I lost fair and square," Anna broke in, her voice weak. "I'll deal with it. Now, let's get Cinders in here before she loses her nerve."

Erica readily scooted into the exam room to which Anna ushered her. Anna bustled after her, ready to be professional vet, personal life left behind.

Janette and Drew exchanged knowing looks, Janette giving Drew a wink.

Anna steadfastly avoided all talk of dates or the Malory brothers while she examined Cinders and quickly vaccinated her, happy to give the cat a clean bill of health. She kept up a running chatter about the B&B as she walked Drew and Erica out the door, then quickly beckoned in the next patient. Janette was still laughing.

The drive back home was lovely—sun shining in a blue sky dotted with clouds, green hills sweeping to the horizon. Beautiful. Not a traffic jam in sight.

A BMW sedan waited in the drive next to the garage when Drew pulled in. As Drew stopped her little car, which looked like a dilapidated antique next to the sleek BMW, a woman emerged, as sleek as her car. She wore a black linen business skirt suit with a white blouse, and had long shapely legs and blond hair.

"Hello there," she said with barely a trace of Texas accent. "You're Drew? I'm Karen Marvin. Ray sent me. He said we need to talk."

Chapter Six

❧❀❧

R ay?" Drew repeated, hoping she didn't sound like an
idiot. "I haven't seen him in a few days."

Drew's clothes were dusty and paint-splotched, and now
covered with cat hair from helping Erica load Cinders into
her new soft-sided cat carrier. Karen, in her spotless suit and
perfect hair, looked like a supermodel turned successful
businesswoman.

The woman's answering look was as poised as the rest of
her. "Ray's a busy man. He told me all about your predicament." She waved a slender hand at the house, one silver ring
clasping her finger. "It's what I do, honey. Help work mira-
cles." She gave Drew a wise look then broke into a surpris-
ingly friendly grin. "I love saying that. Let's go someplace less
hot and dusty and have some iced tea or something. But you
have no idea what I'm talking about, do you? Ray can be a
little cryptic."

She sounded as though she knew Ray well, and Drew's
dart of jealousy dismayed her. She'd only recently met the
man—he could have six girlfriends and a wife for all she

knew. Okay, maybe not, because she was sure someone in town would have told her already.

"Come on." Karen motioned to the garage. Erica openly stared Karen, but she darted inside with Cinders, crooning to the cat still in the carrier.

Once they entered the apartment at the top, Erica banging into her bedroom to release Cinders, Karen made her way to the living room window, glancing around with cool appraisal.

Drew ducked into the bathroom to wash hands and face then returned to the kitchen to fetch the iced tea she'd brewed this morning out of the refrigerator. A full pitcher, in case Ray came by and needed something to drink.

"It's not for sale," Drew said as she poured. "My grandfather's trust is very specific. I can't sell until I have it up and running."

Karen turned. "Oh, I don't want to buy it, honey. I'm not into real estate. At least, not anymore. No, I'm on the board of AGCT Enterprises." She waited while Drew finished pouring tea and brought out an ice tray, but when Drew didn't answer, Karen shook her head. "You haven't heard of it? Ray really needs to open his mouth more. Not that I don't love a dark, handsome, silent type. My current sweetie likes to talk, mostly about himself, though his body makes up for his incessant chatter. Ray now—*mmm, mmm.*"

Drew dropped ice cubes noisily into the glasses. "What is AG ... whatever you said ... Enterprises?"

"AGCT." Karen moved to the counter where Drew placed the glasses and lifted one, ice cubes clinking. "It's a charitable organization, started by the Campbell family to help local businesses. A way to keep the big developers out and family-owned stores in. I run it for them. The Campbells are stunt riders—except Ross, who's trying to be elected sheriff. The Campbells are some beautiful men, my friend. But also smart, with big hearts."

She had a thing for good-looking guys, Drew surmised. She wondered how many had succumbed to Karen's slick beauty. "Are you offering to help me with the B&B?"

"*Maybe* offering. I need to do some research, of course, on the value of the property, the cost of fixing it up." Her voice took on a businesslike tone. "We don't want to pour money into a black hole. I also need to assess your dedication to the project and what *you* bring to the table. We can help but won't do all the work for you."

"And you don't want me taking whatever money and running off into the sunset," Drew finished for her. "I understand."

Karen's hard-as-nails expression abated. "From what Ray says there's not much chance of you doing that, or quitting halfway through. If you did, you'd have to pay the money back."

Drew felt a qualm—there already was a lot at stake. "What if I can pay nothing back? What are the terms of this loan?"

Karen delicately sipped iced tea, her slim fingers embracing the glass. "Not a loan. A grant. We can do loans as well, but I'd wait on that until you have a chance to make money on the B&B. The grant can cover materials, labor, that sort of thing. So you don't max out your credit cards." Karen's raised brows told Drew she suspected that was already the case.

"I can't lie. Money would be truly helpful right now."

"Good. I can get your application started today, if you'd like. I haven't discussed this with the Campbells yet—won't until I finish my research. I'll need your personal information as well. Will you be free tomorrow ..." Karen set down her tea and whipped out her phone, scrolling through it with her fingertips. "Say two-thirty?"

"Sure, that sounds great." Drew had no other appointments, for anything, for the foreseeable future. A great big blank, filled with a ton of physical labor and hair pulling.

"All right, you are scheduled." Karen tapped the phone. "I'll send you a reminder."

"Thank you." Drew breathed out in some hope. If Karen and this charity *could* give her a grant, she might actually have a chance at making this work.

"Thank Ray." Karen slid her phone into her very expensive black leather purse. "I'd heard about your predicament, but didn't know the extent of it. I'm not a Riverbend native, as you can probably guess, so I didn't know much about Paresky and the B&B. He apparently loved the place."

"Apparently." Drew gazed out at the house that now always filled her view. "He could have sold it—I wonder why he never did."

Karen shrugged. "People can be funny about family homes. I've never had one, so I wouldn't know."

Did Drew detect a hint of wistfulness? Hard to say. Karen was incongruous in a town where most people wore jeans and boots, or shorts and casual wear. The climate was warm, and bare legs and sandals abounded.

Why would Karen, who'd be right at home in a Chicago skyscraper, move to the middle of nowhere? Or if she'd come here because of business, family, or friends—why stay? Was she running from things, like Drew?

Karen sipped more iced tea and gave Drew a cool smile,

not about to impart her secrets. "Well, I'll leave you to it. See you tomorrow. No need to walk down with me."

She waved her fingers and strolled out, stepping carefully on her high heels.

"She's pretty," Erica said as they watched from the window. Karen gracefully entered her car and just as gracefully drove it away. "What was she talking about, grants and stuff? What's a grant?"

"It means she might give us money to fix up the house." Drew felt a nugget of hope. "No guarantees, but maybe. Fingers crossed."

Erica made a show of crossing all her fingers, wrapping her thumb around the others. "Toes too."

Drew pulled her daughter into an impulsive hug. "Are you all right, Erica?" She released her and looked into her eyes. "With being here, I mean? You haven't said much about it in the last couple days."

Erica did a quick shrug. "Well, we have Cinders now, and Ray's really nice, and I might get to take horseback riding lessons. I guess it's okay."

Drew squeezed her again. "Everything will we fine, sweetie. When you start school, you'll see."

Erica wrinkled her nose. "Then you had to go and ruin everything by saying the S word."

"I know. I'm evil that way." A flash outside caught her attention, and her heart leapt high. "Oh, it's Ray."

Why did her hands go straight to her hair, and why did she rush to the bathroom and its mirror? She was pathetic.

Erica watched with wry humor. "You look great, Mom. Even with paint in your hair."

Drew scrubbed at the white patch but gave up. "I need to thank him." She babbled the words, hardly knowing what she said, as she slammed out the door, her feet carrying her swiftly down the stairs and out into the bright afternoon.

———

THE SIGHT OF DREW HURRYING OUT THE DOOR TO HIM MADE Ray's blood warm. She'd dressed in jeans and much-stained sneakers for working, a T-shirt that had seen better days already splattered with paint and spackling. She'd caught her dark hair in a ponytail, which emphasized the shape of her face and fine blue eyes.

Ray had tried to stay away the last few days, telling himself he needed to attend to ranch business and not wear out his welcome with Drew.

Today, he'd given up making himself stay home. His excuse for coming was that Fuller had a new shipment of paints, and maybe she'd like to pick out some colors.

Drew jogged to Ray at the back of his truck where he'd started to unload more supplies, plus a couple crowbars to help them pull up rotted boards inside the house.

"Thank you!" she cried as she reached him, sincerity in her voice. "Karen Marvin stopped by. Said you sent her—that she and her nonprofit might be able to fund me." Her smile broadened, gladness in her eyes. "That was so nice of you, Ray."

He'd wanted to make her smile—and there it was. Wide, red-lipped. Beautiful.

Aw, what the hell? Ray emptied his hands of all but his gloves, stepped to Drew, cupped her face, and leaned down to kiss her.

Drew froze a moment in pure surprise, then her fingers

bit down on his arms, and she kissed him back with enthusiasm.

Sunshine warmed them, spreading heat through Ray and making him move even closer to her. They stood against each other, Drew's soft body against his firm one, the sweetness of her soaking into his bones.

She parted her lips, letting him taste her, hand sliding from his arms to his waist. Ray's need spiked, the kisses suddenly not enough.

They'd never be enough, he realized. Not with her. He wanted all of her, to explore her, taste her heat, hear her groan his name in the depths of the night. Drew was beautiful, unexpected, and what he longed for.

Her lips carried fire, even more than when they'd kissed inside the house. That had been from shock and adrenaline, gratitude that they hadn't been hurt.

This was more natural, two people enjoying a kiss under blue sky.

He pulled her a little closer, rewarded by her lips softening to his, her tongue slipping into his mouth and tangling with his. She tasted sweet, like one of Grace's pastries. He'd brought more with him today. Least he could do.

Drew jerked, and Ray knew the magical moment was ending. She broke the kiss but didn't release him, staring up at him with hunger in her eyes.

"Erica," she whispered.

Ray cast a glance at the garage, but Erica was nowhere in sight, not even at the window. "She might not have seen."

"It's okay if she did. She likes you. But ..."

There was always a *but*. Ray brushed Drew's cheek with one gloved finger. "I just wanted to kiss you, is all. We can leave it there."

He did not want to leave it there, no way in hell. He wanted to be with this woman, to make her laugh, to kiss her, to take her to his bed. The attraction to her was strong.

Didn't mean she'd throw herself into his arms and beg him never to go, but maybe they could have something. For a little while at least.

Drew nodded as she studied his face, as though searching for something.

"I guess we'd better get to work," she said.

"That's actually what I came here for." Ray tried to make his voice light. "Really."

"And I am so grateful to you for talking to Karen. Really."

They kept staring at each other. Ray knew right then that having something with her for a little while wouldn't be fulfilling enough. Ever. The more he got to know Drew, the more he'd need of her.

The thought should scare him, but for some reason it made Ray's heart speed in anticipation and hope. He hadn't felt this alive in years, and he wasn't about to shut down the feeling. Not until he found out where this could go.

BY THE TIME DARKNESS FELL, RAY, DREW, AND ERICA WERE tired, dusty, hot, and had collapsed on the sofa—the floor in Erica's case—imbibing cold bottles of water. Erica sprawled on the bare wood with arms outstretched, and Cinders pawed at her shoulder, trying to figure out a way to get underneath her.

"I'm way too tired to cook," Drew announced. She sat enticingly close to Ray, but he'd decided, after his spontaneous kiss, to avoid touching her. He didn't trust himself, even with Erica to chaperone.

"You don't have to," he told her. "I can drive us into town to the diner. Mrs. Ward has her harvest pies now—you've never tasted anything so good."

Erica perked up. "Can we, Mom? I'm so hungry."

"You can't have pie for dinner."

"For *dessert*." Erica rolled her eyes. "Promise. I'll even eat a vegetable. Maybe a green bean. One."

Drew chuckled, but she shook her head. "You don't have to take us anywhere, Ray. You have a life. A home. A brother."

"Not tonight. Kyle's out on his date with Dr. Anna." The house would be dark and empty, the once lively home now too quiet. "We can go talk about them. Everyone else is."

"That's right. Her assistant mentioned it." Drew's amusement showed, but still she hesitated. She was shy, he guessed, reluctant to meet a town that stared so frankly at her. Ray couldn't blame her.

"Dr. Anna is pretty," Erica announced. "And so smart. Your brother should marry her."

"Jumping the gun a little," Ray said. "I'm just glad they finally agreed to sit down at a dinner table together. Let's take it one thing at a time."

"Well, I'm not afraid to sit at a dinner table with you, Ray." Erica leapt to her feet. "Or a *diner* table. Please, Mom. It would be easier if we went with Ray. He knows everyone."

Ray watched Drew run through arguments in her head, and at last decide that her daughter was right.

"Okay," she said but with a cautious note. "But we won't stay long."

"Yay! Washing face now."

Erica ran in to the bathroom. Drew, as though she didn't

want to be left alone with Ray, followed her. She shut the door, and Ray heard some splashing and much laughter.

He made do with washing his hands and face in the kitchen sink, cleaning up his mess with paper towels. He had a change of shirts down in the truck, and no one minded work-stained cowboys in the diner.

Ray was glad he'd cleaned out the truck's cab before he'd come over today. Erica had plenty of room to scramble into the small bench seat in the back once Ray lifted her in. Drew ascended quickly to the front passenger seat, avoiding touching Ray.

"I've never been in a pickup before," Erica announced as Ray climbed into his seat and started up.

"You don't have pickups in Chicago?" Ray asked, as though amazed.

"Of course we do. And a lot of SUVs. But they're hard to park so a lot of people have smaller cars. No one we know has a pickup anyway."

"We like them out here," Ray said. "I can take this one almost anywhere—high clearance, great for off-road or bad weather."

"Do you get bad weather?" Erica sounded eager.

"Sometimes." Ray gazed at the clear evening sky as he pulled out from the B&B, the just-fallen darkness bursting with evening stars, the hills black beneath. "Thunderstorms and such in the summer. Not as bad as North or West Texas, though."

"Chicago weather truly sucks. Just when you think summer is starting, we have a *blizzard*. I won't miss that."

Drew listened without comment and looked relieved when Erica said the last.

The drive to Riverbend was pretty from this side of it,

gentle hills and ranch land lined with fences. Up ahead, the lights of the little town beckoned them on. After a couple miles, Ray glided into Riverbend and around the town square to Mrs. Ward's diner.

The diner parking lot was mostly full, only a few spaces left. As Ray squeezed the truck into a place, reluctance stole over him. For some reason, he didn't want to share Drew with the rest of town—as though what he had with her was special and private.

Or maybe it was fear, that when River County guys saw how great Drew was, they'd go for her. He'd have to step back and let Drew make the choice, because he wasn't a possessive asshole.

Or maybe he'd just never met anyone he'd wanted to possess.

Ray turned off the truck and ushered out Drew and Erica, and they walked together to the diner. Ray led the way in, then he halted, wanting to swear in dismay.

The whole town was here, or near enough. On the other side of the diner was his brother, Kyle, sitting in a booth across from Dr. Anna.

What the hell were *they* doing here? It was supposed to be their date night at Chez Orleans, which was up near White Fork. The two wore dressy clothes that looked a bit worse for wear, but they were *here*.

Even worse, Christina Campbell, Ray's ex-girlfriend, stood in the aisle next to Anna and Kyle, all three turning around to gaze at Drew with interest. Christina's daughter, Emma, bounced in her arms, waving her chubby hands.

"Hi!" Emma yelled.

Chapter Seven

❧

Drew felt every eye on her as she followed Ray to a booth, the entire town assessing her, trying to peel back the layers of her life to have a good look.

With some relief, she recognized Dr. Anna and lifted her hand in greeting when Anna waved at her. Anna wore a nice blue dress that was out of place in a diner full of jeans, shorts, T-shirts, and tank tops. The man across from her, who looked so much like Ray she knew he was his brother, was likewise incongruous in a suit.

The leggy woman in shorts standing next to them, holding a child obviously her daughter, was very pretty, with curly black hair, dark eyes, and a smile that matched the one on the little girl's face.

Ray didn't greet anyone. He quickly slid into the booth and picked up the menu, holding it in front of his face like he'd never seen it before. Erica imitated him, her eyes widening at the pictures of plump burgers and massive fries.

The leggy woman strode over with determination, and the whole diner watched her, avidly interested.

"Hi!" the little girl in her arms bellowed, waving a fist.

"Hi there," Erica greeted the child as the woman halted by their table. "I'm Erica. What's your name?"

"Emma." The mite looked proud.

"Very nice to meet you," Erica said.

She and Emma were the only ones oblivious to the tension. The woman stared frankly at Drew, and Ray lowered his menu.

"Christina," he said in a half growl.

Christina ignored him and addressed Drew. "Dr. Anna says you're Drew Paresky, and that you're restoring the B&B. Very cool. Welcome to Riverbend."

"Thank you."

The air between Ray and Christina was charged, which made Drew's heart constrict. She'd been around the block a few times and knew exactly what the strain meant—they had once been a couple.

Ray's cheekbones were red but he strove to be polite. "How you doing, Emma?"

Emma looked delighted. "Hi!" She waved at him.

"She's doing great," Christina answered for her. "Thanks."

"I'm glad." Ray's answer was sincere. He pulled his gaze from Christina and rested it on Drew.

The minute their eyes met, Ray's mouth softened, his expression understanding. He knew she knew, and he was apologizing for the scene.

Which wasn't even a scene. Everyone was as polite as could be.

Christina switched her focus back to Drew. "You're from a real city. With department stores and fashionable clothes and everything. I've always wanted to go to Chicago."

"It can be fun," Drew said. "And crowded and dirty and cold. Or hot. It's pretty here."

"It is. River County is the most beautiful place in the world, in my opinion." Christina's eyes shone. "But sometimes the most boring place in the world. The only interesting things going on right now are, one: you moving here. That's why everyone's staring at you. Sorry about that. We're not rude—we just don't have anything else to do. Two: Kyle and Dr. Anna."

She glanced at Kyle and Anna who gazed at each other awkwardly as they took bites of their respective burgers.

"They were supposed to go to Chez Orleans," Ray said in a rumble. "Did my brother screw up and lose the directions?"

"You didn't hear?" Christina looked surprised, as though town news reached everyone by osmosis. "Sherrie Duncan got run off the road—Kyle and Anna stopped to help. She had an overturned horse trailer with one of her horses trapped inside. Everyone, including the horse, is okay and back home, but Anna's and Kyle's nice clothes aren't so nice anymore, and they decided to come here instead."

"That's terrible." Drew's sympathy emerged. "I'm glad the woman and her horse are okay. Dr. Anna was so nervous about this date. She must be disappointed … or maybe relieved. Hard to tell."

"Right now they're debating whether they need a do-over." Christina's smile flashed, making her more beautiful still. "This will be fun to watch."

Christina seemed friendly enough and truly interested in Drew, behaving in no way like a jealous ex, plus she had a gorgeous baby on her hip. Whatever she'd had with Ray was over, it looked like, and Christina had moved on. Drew wondered if Ray had.

"Since Ray isn't the voluble type, I'll make the introduc-
tions," Christina said. "I'm Christina Campbell, married to
Grant—there's five Campbell brothers so don't worry if you
can't remember all their names at first."

Campbell, as in the family with the nonprofit that helped
out local businesses. Drew didn't mention this, as Karen had
said she wanted to wait before she brought it up with the
Campbells.

Erica listened with interest. "Is Faith your niece?" she
asked. "I've already lost track."

Christina laughed. "I don't blame you. Faith is Carter's
daughter, and Ray's sister married him."

"Faith is going to give me riding lessons. I think."

More interest entered Christina's eyes. "She'd love to. Tell
you what—why don't you head over to the ranch tomorrow?
Circle C, on the southwest side of town. Faith will be home,
and she's dying to meet you."

Erica swung to Drew. "Can I, Mom? Say yes."

"Carter and Grace will take good care of Erica," Ray said,
confident. "No worries about that."

"I think it will be all right," Drew said. Erica needed to
meet girls her age and do something besides work on the
B&B and miss her friends. "She's never been near horses,
though."

Erica put on her *Oh, Mom*, face but said nothing.

"She won't be able to say that for long," Christina said.
"Faith is already a champion rider and a great teacher. Grace
will be there too, to watch out for her, and probably bake her
a ton of treats."

"We miss Grace," Ray said nostalgically. "Kyle and I have
lost ten pounds each since she left."

"Yeah, because you both were so tubby before." Christina

gave Drew a wry look. "You'll have to come over soon too, Drew. For a Campbell family dinner. Not that you'll get a word in edgewise, but the Campbell brothers will do plenty of talking for you."

"The women of that family can sure go on too," Ray said. "Don't put all the blame on the guys. I'm not excluding my sweet baby sister."

"I won't argue. Bailey—she's married to Adam—is *my* sister, so we get into sister stuff. Ross just married Callie, and she was a debutante, so she keeps us all under control now. She's poised, beautiful, and smart. And you can't hate her, because she's so damned *nice*."

Ray let out a chuckle, relaxing. "Keeps you all under control. Right. Where's Grant tonight? Haven't seen him around much."

"He and Tyler are putting together a new show, so they're training a lot. They're stunt riders," she said to Drew. "I was hungry and didn't want to wait for them." She glanced at the waitress, who moved determinedly toward the table. "I guess that's why you're here too. Well, I'll leave you to it. Erica, show up about lunchtime—I'll tell Faith to expect you. See you then."

"See you. Thanks," Erica gushed.

Christina said, "You're welcome, sweetie," and walked away, her daughter shouting a "Hi!" at the next person she saw.

"She's really nice," Erica informed Ray.

Ray shrugged. "Yeah, she is. I'll have a burger." This to the waitress, who hovered.

Drew ordered a roast beef sandwich and Erica had a burger—"The one Ray's having," she declared.

Drew was dying to ask all about Christina and her past

with Ray, but she knew this was not the time or place. Christina had seemed contented enough, and Drew had seen the love in her eyes when she'd spoken her husband's name and looked at the daughter she'd had with him.

The fact that Ray had not mentioned the woman at all in the week he'd been helping Drew could mean he was over her. Drew had dated men who *hadn't* been over their breakups or divorces, and it had been very obvious.

But then, Ray wasn't like any other guy she'd gone out with. He didn't slop his emotions onto her, didn't talk about anything emotional at all, in fact. He had easy silences, speaking only when he needed to. Refreshing.

Ray caught her eye. He had to know she was curious, but he only toyed with his glass of iced tea the waitress brought, and started talking about what they should take apart on the house next.

AT THE MALORY RANCH THE NEXT MORNING, RAY WATCHED their trainer take a new cutting horse through some moves— quick halt, swift changes of leads—and tried to ignore his brother next to him.

Kyle had left his walking stick in the house, a good sign he was better, but his newfound energy had also reawakened his obnoxious curiosity.

"So, who is this Drew?" Kyle asked without preliminary.

Ray made a slight shrug, tamping down his irritation. "I'm sure everyone in the diner told you about her. Why ask me?"

"Because *you* were the one having dinner with her."

Ray knew damn well the whole diner had eagerly watched the encounter between him and Christina and Drew. They were probably all talking about it this morning, like Kyle was now.

"*You* were having dinner with Dr. Anna," Ray answered with a growl. "Believe me, that was way more interesting."

"Everyone knows about Anna's bet with me. But we don't know about you and Drew Paresky."

"See? You know her name." *Now, let it go.*

"Anna told me. She treated their cat."

Ray gave him a nod. "Cinders, yeah."

Kyle stared as though he'd bore into Ray's head. "Cinders?"

"Because we found her in the fireplace."

Kyle planted his booted foot on the bottom rail. "*We? Okay, so you know their cat's name and you found it with them. While I've never heard about any of this."

"You've been busy. How's Anna?"

Kyle's flush told Ray Anna wasn't far from Kyle's mind. Ray wondered what had happened after the pair of them had left the diner last night. Anna had paid for her own meal, a fact that got talked about up and down the aisles once Kyle and Anna had departed.

"She's fine," Kyle answered with a grunt. "What you been up to? Haven't seen you around here much."

Ray scowled. "Have I let the ranch go to shit? No. Then what's the deal? I have my own life."

Kyle's gaze didn't waver. "You seeing her?"

Ray ran out of patience. "I can see her—I have eyes. But no, we're not going out or engaged or secretly married. Drew needs to turn around the B&B, and I'm helping her out."

Would Kyle give it a rest? No, he sucked in a breath to ask another question, but fortunately, Kyle's cell phone rang.

Ray saw Anna's name flash on the screen. Kyle turned away and planted the phone to his ear so fast that Ray had to chuckle. Kyle had it bad for Dr. Anna. As soon as he figured that out and left Ray alone, the better.

Ray watched the training, giving advice from time to time, until the session finished. After that, he went to the office and told Margaret he was going out for the day. Wasn't certain when he'd return. Margaret gave him her keen-eyed look, and Ray beat a hasty retreat.

By the time he reached Drew's B&B, his heart was lighter. He liked coming out here—his worries faded as he drove the few miles, as did his loneliness. Drew and Erica were filling a place in his life he hadn't realized was so empty.

Drew wasn't home. Her car, usually left outside the garage, was gone, and Ray remembered she'd taken Erica to the Campbell ranch to meet Faith.

Shouldn't keep him from getting to work. Ray had sheet-rocked and painted the whole garage and had started on refinishing the garage floor. That was almost done—next he'd replace all the shelving and cabinetry they'd torn out. This would be a garage to die for when he was done, and a nice storage space for Drew.

He'd already done one coat of epoxy on the floor, and now he mixed up the parts in the can, got out the roller brush and applied the second coat. Drew pulled up outside when he was halfway done, and she waved at him as she went up the stairs to the apartment, carefully avoiding the wet step he'd coated.

Ray finished, cleaned up the stuff and himself at the water

spigot, and went upstairs. He found Drew painting the bathroom, standing inside the tub to reach the wall above it.

"Great time to do this with Erica gone for the day," she said as Ray leaned on the bathroom doorframe. "She was so excited to see the horses, and Faith seems like a sweet girl."

"She is."

Drew had paint in her hair, the pale pink she'd chosen. Not too pink, because if this would be the honeymoon suite, she'd said, she didn't want the groom to run away screaming. Keep the color subtle but romantic.

"Garage floor just needs to dry," Ray said as Drew continued to roller paint on the wall. "Then I'll rinse it off, and you can park inside instead of leaving your car out in the weather. The cabinets will be great in there once those are done."

"Uh huh."

Scintillating conversation. Ray had never been one for poetic words, but he suddenly wished he could banter and charm like Kyle or Tyler Campbell. Ray was the silent type, more like Carter, but sometimes being quiet meant life passed you by.

"Hope you weren't overwhelmed by the Campbells," he tried. "When we were kids, we fought all the time. Me and Kyle against the five of them. Well, mostly me and Kyle against Adam, Grant, and Carter. Tyler and Ross kind of stayed on the sidelines."

"They told me." Drew applied the roller with vigor. "And that you're all friends now."

"More or less. Grace has been a good peacemaker."

"They also told me all about you and Christina." More rollering, droplets of pink splattering to Drew's hair, face, and the bathtub. "They all seemed to think I needed to know."

She sounded bright, even cheerful—too much so—and she wouldn't look at Ray.

Ray covered the roller handle, stopping it. "Maybe you should hear my side of the story."

When Drew finally looked at him, her face was stiff. "No need. None of my business."

She tried to get on with painting, but Ray took the roller firmly away from her. Drew began a startled protest, but Ray pulled her to him over the bathtub's lip, wrapped her in his arms, and kissed her.

Chapter Eight

Ray's kiss was strong, pushing them both back until Drew touched the painted wall. She didn't care. His warmth surrounded her, taking away all her doubt.

What Christina, Bailey, and Grace had told her, reassuring her over and over, was that Ray's brief relationship with Christina was long over. Worry about it flowed away now with Ray's kiss. The past didn't matter. Ray was here, with Drew, and real.

He took his time kissing her, his mouth parting her lips, tongue sliding against hers. His hands rested solidly on her back, not letting her fall.

The kiss robbed her of breath, weakened her knees. But it didn't matter, because Ray held her up. His mouth was skilled, the scrape of his whiskers and the heat of his breath opening something inside her.

Ray eased back, finally ending the kiss, but he stayed close, as though he didn't want to let her go. Drew touched his cheek, meeting his liquid green gaze.

"I should ask for help painting more often," she whispered.

"You didn't ask."

The roller had ended up in the roller tray, which rested across the sink.

"But maybe I should."

Ray grinned, lighting his face.

He made Drew want to joke, to laugh. It had been so long since she'd shared laughter with anyone but Erica.

Ray tore off a paper towel and applied it to her hair, which must be full of paint. "I think we need to talk."

"Uh oh. Never good words." Drew touched his face again, liking the faint burn of his whiskers. "How about we just kiss?"

Heat flickered in Ray's eyes. "Sounds good. But while Erica is out …"

Drew sighed, resigned. In her experience, long conversations about life never ended well. Philip had enjoyed family conferences, which were mostly to go over Drew's supposed shortcomings, including detailed instructions on how she could improve. His brother, Jules, had the same tendencies.

She let Ray lead her into the living room, mostly because she liked his strong hand in hers, but forestalled him as they sat down.

"You don't have anything to explain to me, Ray. Your past, your relationships, are your business. I'm the stranger here, and what you did before I arrived has nothing to do with me."

Ray waited, patient as always, until she finished, his green eyes holding mysteries.

"I don't want you looking at me like you did at the diner, always wondering." He hadn't released her hand and now he twined his fingers through hers. "Grant and Christina fell madly in love the minute they started going out—Grant had just graduated high school and Christina was a few years older. But they fought all the time too, and when they broke up some years later, everyone figured that was it, they were just too volatile to make it. I took a chance and asked Christina out. I didn't expect a grand romance, wasn't pining for her or anything like that. I just thought we could have some fun. But I could tell that, no matter what, she was still into Grant. I mean, *really* into him. Couldn't take her eyes off him when he was around. He'd try to make her jealous, and she'd do the same. I got tired of being the piece of meat in the middle. When we broke it off, it was a relief. My ego was hurt, yeah, but it was peaceful to go back to riding bulls. Way less dangerous." A smile crinkled the corners of his eyes.

It amazed Drew that Christina hadn't seen Ray's worth. Drew had met Grant today, who was hot, there was no question—he and Christina had a chemistry that zinged off the pair of them.

But if the choice had been Drew's it would have been easy to make. Grant was cute, but there was something about Ray. Grant was a swiftly moving river—Ray was deep, still water Drew wanted to explore.

Drew squeezed his hand. "Her loss."

"There's a little bit more. I want you to know before you hear it from gossip. Maybe you already have."

Drew had sensed there was more today at the Campbells, perceived they'd been falling all over each other to *not* say anything.

"Go ahead," she said, keeping her voice light. "I won't throw you down the stairs. You're too big."

His lips twitched but his eyes remained serious, worried, which worried Drew.

"Thing is," Ray said slowly. "Christina dumped me and then was with Grant again real fast. I mean, same-day fast. Maybe even before she and I split, I'm not sure. Then she found out she was pregnant with Emma, and there was a time she wasn't sure ..."

He trailed off and swallowed, embarrassed.

"Which of you was the dad," Drew finished, a lump rising in her throat. "Emma looks a lot like Grant."

"Grant's her daddy, no question. We did a DNA test, and Grant was the clear winner. I'd figured that, but Christina wanted us all to know for sure. Only fair."

"I'm sorry." Drew saw in Ray's eyes that while he shrugged off the incident, it had haunted him for a while. "As a mom, I know what it feels like to be told you're having a kid. Scary, but so wonderful at the same time, right?"

"Yeah." Ray nodded. "It would have messed things up for all of us, but yeah, for a time, I kinda hoped." He gave her a quiet look. "That's weird, but I couldn't help it."

"I don't think it's weird."

She wasn't sure how she felt, knowing Ray had shared something so intimate with Christina. Envious, definitely. Plus a little anger at Christina for racing from Ray to Grant, and causing Ray anguish. Ray would never say the word "anguish," but she saw the flash of it.

She'd also seen how much Grant and Christina loved each other, and how much they adored their daughter. They belonged together, that family. But Ray had been pushed out in the cold.

As Drew had said, Christina's loss.

Ray lifted their twined fingers and kissed Drew's. "Now

it's your turn. I don't need your life history, but tell me if Erica's daddy will show up and wonder what I'm doing in his wife's living room."

"He won't." Drew paused, waiting for the hollow pain and guilt that always accompanied thoughts of Philip, but to her surprise, she felt only a flutter. "Philip was killed eight years ago, in an accident during a snowstorm. Huge pileup in a whiteout, and he wasn't the only casualty. It was horrible. We'd already separated, had agreed to divorce." She paused. "*Agreed* isn't a good word. I left him. Kind of the same thing you were saying—a relief when it was over. I finally could eat breakfast without being criticized about every bite."

Drew remembered the days after she'd packed her bags and Erica's and walked away. Nothing had been easy. When Philip finally figured out she was serious he'd turned a cold shoulder, saying she'd come crawling back home before long.

It had been hard not to—money was tight, and Erica didn't understand why her father wasn't there anymore. Philip's derision had sounded in Drew's head whenever she ate white bread instead of whole grain, had an extra slice of bacon, or lingered over her coffee.

His admonishing voice had taken a long time to go away. Six months after Drew had taken this step, Philip had decided to drive to Wisconsin to visit a woman he'd met at a conference. A storm had struck, as they could so fast in that part of the country, and he'd died.

"His brother blamed me," Drew said quietly. "If I hadn't broken up with Philip, Jules said, he wouldn't have been going to visit another woman that night. What Jules doesn't understand is there's no guarantee he wouldn't have made the drive that night to visit the woman anyway. I suspect he enjoyed himself at his conferences quite a lot. He never took me."

"His choice to go," Ray said. "That can't be your fault."

"It wasn't." Drew dragged in a breath. "But it was a long time before I could throw off that certainty. We screw ourselves up."

"We sure do."

They sat in silence a moment, Ray tracing one finger over Drew's palm, which sent nice tingles through her.

"When I heard I'd inherited this house, I didn't think very long before I decided to accept it," Drew said after a time. "There were too many things I needed to leave behind." She glanced around at the drop cloths, inhaled the smells of paint, varnish, and drying epoxy downstairs. "Not necessarily a *practical* choice."

Ray continued to caress her palm. "We're making a dent. Little bit at a time, and it gets done."

Drew relaxed into a smile. "You're such a philosopher."

"Nah. Training horses takes a lot of patience. So does learning to sit on a bull who doesn't want you there. Not to mention being the oldest brother of three wild siblings. Well, two wild ones and Grace. But Grace was so nice to people, no matter how bad they were, that it scared me to death. I was always trying to protect her."

"She seems very happy now."

"Yep. Carter was one of the bad people, but he was ever gentle with Grace." Ray softened. "Now if we can get Kyle to move his butt with Dr. Anna, that will be another sibling taken care of. I think Lucy's okay, but she's kind of swept away her old life for her new."

"Like I'm doing."

"Sort of. But Lucy's got family and friends here, whenever

she wants them. You didn't leave that behind, I'm getting from what you're saying."

"No." Drew again waited for the worry about leaving her job, the apartment she'd known for a long time, her neighbors, the shop on the corner where she'd grab a quick coffee, to manifest and eat at her. It didn't come. She'd have to think about why not. "I liked my job and the people I worked with, but I didn't have—I don't know. Roots. I might be looking for that here."

"Your grandparents were Riverbenders. So here—roots." Ray gestured around them.

Drew wanted to laugh. "In the most basic way." She rubbed a hand through her hair. "Will this work? And even if we do fix up the house, will anyone come to stay in it? I don't see a ton of tourists running through Riverbend."

"Oh, they're out here," Ray said. "Once they know you have a great place for them to take a load off, they'll come."

Drew rested her other hand on their twined ones. "Anyone ever tell you you're a nice guy?"

"No." Ray gazed at her, deadpan. "They say *Ray's the mean one. Watch out for him.*"

"No way."

"Way."

They looked at each other a while, words trailing away. Drew never felt the urgent need to think of something—anything—to say when she was with Ray. They could work in silence or drink iced tea and simply gaze across the land, enjoying the sunshine and occasional cool breeze.

Drew realized how alone they were. Erica's absence made the place so quiet, every click of the refrigerator or the wet slather of Cinders licking her fur on the windowsill loud in the stillness.

They were alone, no one to interrupt, no one to judge. Drew's bedroom would be bathed in sunshine, the bed spread with crisp sheets.

A glance at Ray let her know he was thinking about it too. They could lie together while Drew explored his body, discovering whether the muscles under his clothes were as taut and smooth as the ones he bared. She wondered how gentle his big hands would be on her body, and if she could keep from wrapping herself around him and taking her fill.

Her face grew hot, and Ray looked away, clearing his throat. The silence became suddenly less soothing.

"Guess we should get to work," Ray said.

Drew nodded. "Guess we should."

"Guy from White Fork is driving out a load of lumber. I'm going to replace all the boards and beams on the porch so we can actually walk there."

"Thanks for arranging that."

Drew reminded herself that her purpose was to fix the house, fulfill the terms of the trust, and then decide what to do. Rolling in bed with a hot cowboy was *not* on the agenda.

As Ray released her hand and rose to his feet, sauntering to the kitchen to deposit his iced tea glass, Drew's gaze riveted instantly to his nice butt and powerful thighs.

She decided right then that she needed to put the hot cowboy *on* her agenda, and started thinking of the many and interesting ways she could do that.

HARD WORK WAS THE ONLY THING THAT KEPT RAY FROM catching up Drew, running upstairs with her, and having hot, intense sex on her bed. That, and Jack Hillman arriving with the lumber Ray had ordered.

Jack was a biker who made a living with a lumberyard in White Fork, supplying builders and ranchers all over River County with whatever they couldn't get at Fuller's Feed and Hardware. He had connections in the cities and could order just about what anyone wanted.

He, Ray, and Kyle had been friends for years, though Jack had breached the Malory-Campbell rivalry by being friends with Carter as well.

As they discussed how best to gut the house and how much help Drew was going to need, Karen arrived in her fancy car.

Jack cut off the conversation and gazed across the drive at Karen emerging, long legs first, from the low-slung car. Karen had lived in Riverbend a couple years now, but she still dressed in linen skirt suits and high heels, with gold, silver, or diamonds clasping fingers and ears.

"She is something," Jack said to Ray, his admiration obvious.

"She is something scary," Ray answered with a grin. "And likes cowboys barely over the legal age. She's going around with Deke Vernier right now. You know, the dude who can't say two coherent sentences without sounding like a dick."

"Know him." Jack continued to stare at Karen until she glanced behind her and caught both men's gazes on her.

Ray gave her a polite nod, and Karen's lips quirked into a brief smile. Jack did nothing, said nothing. He only stared, until Karen stiffened and swung away. She headed for the stairs of the garage, every line of her frosty.

"You serious?" Ray asked as Jack continued to watch the

door through which she'd disappeared. "You're way older than her type. And you don't ride horses or bulls."

"I think she maybe needs a taste of something different."

The determination on Jack's face made Ray want to laugh. He didn't know if Karen had just met her match, or Jack had.

They worked into late afternoon, Jack and his guys lending a hand. Karen, who'd come to talk to Drew about the grant again, departed with her usual easy grace. Jack watched her every step, and Karen pretended not to notice Jack at all.

A Campbell pickup drove in around six to disgorge a tired, dusty, and happy Erica. The driver was Grace.

Grace gave Ray a delighted hug as Erica ran to Drew, talking nonstop about her wonderful day.

"I brought Drew a pan of enchiladas," Grace said, releasing Ray. "Think she'll mind? I figure she doesn't have a lot of time or space to cook here. Oh, and a mess of cupcakes, assorted, that were too many for the bakery."

Grace could have sold the surplus cupcakes quickly at her little bakery on the town square, Ray knew. She'd brought them out of kindness.

"I think Drew would be happy to eat all your food," Ray said. "Did Erica like the horses?"

"Was love at first sight. She's coming back over tomorrow for more riding. I think Faith and Dominic just made a new best friend."

"Good." Ray saw no need to elaborate, but he was glad. Erica was restless and needed kids her own age to be with. Faith would ease her into school next week, which would be a load off Drew's mind.

Grace's smile turned lopsided. "You've been spending a lot of time here, Ray. Lots and lots."

"Ranch is slow," Ray answered quickly. "I'm not doing as much competing this year, and Drew needs help."

"Mmm hmm. Remember how I jumped at the chance to work in the Campbells' kitchen? Said Olivia needed serious help cooking for her sons and their growing families?"

"And Kyle shit his pants. Yeah, I remember."

"Turns out, in my heart, I only wanted to be closer to Carter."

"I know." Ray pinned her with a hard look. "What's your point?"

"I think you know my point." Grace turned serious. "I'm happy for you."

Ray scowled. "There is no guarantee Drew's going to stay once she's done fixing up the B&B, or that she'll be interested in a has-been bull rider except for his skills in hammering and sawing."

Grace put her hands on her hips, giving him the mulish look she had when she'd been little and wrapping her big brothers around her finger. "You need to make some effort, Ray. Drew's nice, has a great daughter, and a good heart. I know these things. But she'll run right back north if she doesn't have a reason to stay in Riverbend."

"Maybe. I figure that's her business."

Grace rolled her eyes. "I swear, I'm never going to be able to cook a big holiday dinner for my brothers and their *families*. My sister either. Y'all are so determined to be single."

"Go lecture Kyle. He's the one falling all over himself with Anna."

Grace's impish smile returned. "I know. Isn't it fun? But at least he's trying. If you like Drew, big brother, act like it. She can't read your mind."

"Thanks for the advice, baby sister. Now go away."

Grace stuck her tongue out at him, not intimidated in the least. "Kyle's going out with Anna again tonight. Finally taking her to Chez Orleans. He even bought a new suit."

"Damn." Ray pretended amazement. "Well, good luck to him."

"You're a shit. See you, Ray." Grace turned away on light feet to her pickup to unload the food she'd brought.

Ray cleaned himself off and helped her. Drew, as predicted, was delighted with the gift and spontaneously invited Ray to stay for dinner, after Grace departed, and help eat it.

You need to make some effort, Ray. Grace's words rang in his head as he dug into the savory enchiladas. Erica both ate and talked nonstop about horses, the Campbells, Grace, Faith, Dominic, and Dodie, the horse she'd ridden.

Ray watched Drew's face soften as she realized how happy Erica was—they'd planted their first shoot here. He thought of the awkwardness earlier today when he and Drew realized they were alone, how he'd silently cursed himself for setting up Jack's delivery for that afternoon.

Grace was right. He needed to fight for Drew, to not let her run back to Chicago and her cold, lonely life there, leaving him cold and lonely here.

She was definitely worth it.

RAY MADE HIMSELF LEAVE AFTER DINNER, BECAUSE HE KNEW that with every passing minute it would be harder and harder to go.

Erica had chattered on through the meal about her riding lesson with Faith, and also Jess's son Dominic, whom

Erica had clicked with, as they'd both grown up in big cities.

"Don't worry, Mom, he's way too young for me," Erica said with twelve-year-old confidence. "But it's nice to talk to someone who understands it's weird not to hear traffic noise."

Erica was tired though—horses could take it out of a person—and she drooped over her last bite of Grace's cupcakes. Drew declared Erica should go to bed, and Ray took that as his cue to leave.

Drew walked him down and said goodbye, her smile as warm as the September evening.

Ray didn't want to go home to his big empty house so he drove into Riverbend and made his way to the bar. Kyle was out with Anna tonight, and if his brother did things right, he'd not be back until very late.

The bar held an after-dinner crowd. Hal Jenkins was there, and Ray spent time catching up with him. Jack Hillman joined them, the three men talking about whatever. The five Campbell brothers, who used to fill this bar, were notably absent. All home with wives and kids now. How times changed.

Karen entered around midnight. She owned the bar and came in to check the books, see how things were going, and chat with her patrons. Tonight she was followed by a glowering Deke, a young bull rider who was a champion and knew it.

"What are we doing here?" Deke demanded as he slid to a barstool near Ray and Jack. He caught the bartender's eye and mimed pulling a draft of beer.

"I work here," Karen answered in a mild tone. "A few minutes in the office, then we'll go."

Deke scowled, already mostly drunk. "You're out with *me*, baby. I don't want to go to no office—unless there's a couch in there."

Karen gave him a beatific smile and patted his cheek. "You're adorable. Unfortunately, I need to finish some paperwork before tomorrow, and the couch is off limits. Only for about twenty minutes, honey."

Deke glared, unhappy to not be the center of her world, but Karen walked away serenely. Deke slurped down half the beer the bartender had poured for him, thumped the mug to the counter, and started for the office door that Karen had closed.

"Time to show that bitch who's the man in this relationship."

"We know who *that* is," someone called. "And it ain't you."

Deke swung around, pointing. "You shut the fuck up."

Howling laughter met his declaration. Deke growled, flushing red, and continued toward the office, clearly ready to take out his frustration on Karen.

Ray got up, but Jack was faster. He blocked Deke's way solidly—no one could be more solid when he wanted than Jack.

"Out of my way," Deke slurred. "Tame your friends, Malory."

"Jack does what he wants," Ray said quietly. "And I think he wants you to leave."

"Like hell." Deke, with a bravery that could only come from too much beer, rushed Jack.

Deke was a rodeo man, young, fit, and used to bar fights, but Jack was a seasoned street fighter. He had Deke spun around in a chokehold before Deke could even blink. Jack kicked Deke's leg out from under him, and the cowboy went down on one knee. Deke struck out with fists, hitting Jack, and incidentally, Ray, who'd come to help.

Ray reached to haul Deke up and drag him to the door, but Jack gave Deke a tight punch to the face, putting Deke out cold.

"How about we take out the trash?" Jack asked Ray, his eyes sparkling with enjoyment.

"What the hell did you *do?*" Karen was there, arms akimbo as she glared first at Jack then Ray, then down at Deke. "Shit, there goes my night."

"He kinda deserved it," Ray pointed out, deciding to play referee. "Called you a bitch."

"Of course he did," Karen snapped. "I am one." She looked straight at Jack. "Will you take Deke home, please? I don't want to deal with him when he wakes up. And make sure he's all right."

Jack regarded her in silence, face blank. Karen gazed back at him, a flush rising. As the entire bar watched, Karen's brittleness softened.

"Please," she said. She reached into her purse and lifted out a keyfob. "Take my car."

Jack kept up his stare for another tense moment then he gave her a nod and closed his fingers around the fob. Karen snatched her hand away quickly, as though afraid to touch him.

Karen marched back into the office, head high, and slammed the door. Jack, in silence, heaved Deke easily over his shoulder and walked out of the bar. A round of applause sounded behind him.

Ray, laughing quietly, followed them out. He helped Jack shove Deke into Karen's back seat, then he waved as Jack drove out. He looked forward to telling the story to Drew.

Ray stood motionless in the middle of the dark parking lot, realizing just how much he looked forward to it. He pictured Drew's eyes lighting with laughter, her cheeks flushing with pleasure. Her delight would be his.

He knew he must be drunk, because Ray sober would never think of a phrase like *her delight would be his.*

No driving home, then. Ross Campbell's deputies would happily pull him over and he didn't need a DUI. Where to go then? In his younger years, he'd call Grace, who would sleepily but happily show up to help out her brother. But Grace was now married to Carter and had kids to stay home with, and he didn't want to bother her.

Jack lived a few streets over. Ray had crashed at his place more than once and knew where the man kept his spare key. Besides, when Jack came back from taking Deke home—or to the trash dump, who knew?—he might want to talk. Or at least have someone to sit in silence with.

Ray kept that goal in mind as he walked carefully through the streets—that is, until he saw his brother's fancy rented car parked in front of Dr. Anna's dark house.

He grinned, hard. At least someone was having fun tonight. He took out his cell phone and dialed without hesitation.

"Drew," he said when she answered groggily. "Want to help me with Kyle and Dr. Anna?"

Chapter Nine

Drew shouldn't be so happy to drive out in the middle of the night in answer to a man's summons.

She should be at home, curled up under blankets enjoying a well-earned sleep. Not driving through darkness, Erica snoozing in the back seat, excited to be meeting Ray for a midnight adventure.

But her heart hammered, her fingers tingled, and she couldn't stop her smiles. Of all the people Ray could have called, he'd decided on her.

She found him where he said he'd be, at the corner of the town square, waiting in the shadow of a doorway.

"Sorry for disturbing you," he said as he climbed into the car, his large physique dwarfing the small seat. "I had a little too much beer, and I'd need a ride home anyway."

His words slurred a bit, but he didn't seem too inebriated. Not that Drew was an expert. Philip had never gotten drunk —he was too perfect for that.

"You want me to drive you home?" Drew asked. She longed to see where Ray lived—at least, more than simply driving past the Malory ranch and looking longingly at the gate.

"Not yet. Go down this street here. It's where Dr. Anna lives. But kill your lights."

Drew turned off the lights, unworried, because there was no other car on the street.

"Park there."

Drew pulled over where Ray pointed. They were in front of a row of houses identical in shape but painted differently, each with neat front lawns. She'd driven down this street before and liked the old bungalows.

A luxury sedan sat in front of a house a few doors down, the only vehicle not securely in a carport or in a driveway alongside its house.

"Come on." Ray got out.

Drew turned off the engine and slid from the car, and Erica, now awake and eager, climbed out from the back.

"What are we doing?" Erica whispered in a hiss that must have carried across town. "Stealing that car? I think that's illegal, Ray."

"Kyle rented it," Ray said. "He's in there, with Dr. Anna." He gestured at the house. The porch light was on, projecting brightness into the night, but the front windows were dark.

"You mean, they're humping?" Erica's whisper rang out.

"Erica!" Drew said, sotto voce. "Go wait in the car."

"Oh, come on, Mom. I know what humping is. Is he going to marry her?"

Instead of answering, Ray motioned them on to the lone car. It was a Lexus, a new one. Ray opened the driver's door —it wasn't locked—and indicated Drew should get in. She did, while Ray went around to the passenger side and Erica hopped into the back. By tacit agreement, they all closed their doors with soft clicks.

"Now what?" Erica asked. "Are we going to sneak up on them? Or wait here and scare Kyle?"

"We're going to take the car back to the rental place," Ray said. "If Anna's neighbors see it still here in the morning, they'll give her hell. Riverbend's a pretty tolerant town, but there's not much else to do but gossip."

"And Dr. Anna will be humiliated," Drew finished.

She thought about how Dr. Anna had gone shy when Janette had teased her about Kyle, how she'd flushed last night in the diner. If it was known Kyle had spent the night, her embarrassment would be acute. That kind of stress might drive her and Kyle apart.

"So we're going to remove the evidence. How?" Drew put her hand to the ignition, but no key dangled there.

"Easy. The rental place gave me a spare when I drove Kyle to White Fork to pick up the car." Ray produced a fob from his pocket. "He was afraid Kyle would lose the key or lock it inside." He grinned. "We didn't tell him."

Drew grabbed key from him and started the car. It purred.

"This is fun," she said. "Where to?"

WITH READY COMPLIANCE, DREW FOLLOWED RAY'S DIRECTIONS to the car dealer in White Fork, cheerful for a woman he'd dragged out of bed.

The Lexus had satellite radio and Drew found an oldies station. She cranked up the volume, and she and Erica sang loudly with the tunes.

"We did this on the way down from Chicago, to stay awake," Drew said in a lull between songs. "A fun way to travel."

Ray had done plenty of long-haul driving from rodeo to rodeo, which became tedious fast. But he'd look forward to the road if he had Drew beside him, singing her heart out.

In too short a time, they'd reached the dealer in White Fork, who'd rented the car to Kyle. The main gates were closed but there was a parking space by the front office.

"Here we are," Drew said as she pulled in and shut off the engine. "Now, how do we get back?"

Ray stared at her, his mind befuddled. "Oh. Yeah."

"I thought you'd set up a ride, genius." Drew laughed at him. "You're usually so efficient and think of everything. Oh, well, I guess we can Uber."

"In River County? Don't think so. But we have Sonny."

"Who's Sonny?" Erica asked, her arm over the front seat.

"He drives our only taxi. His wife doesn't let him go out after midnight, though."

"Seriously?" Erica demanded, and Drew laughed some more.

"It's a big change to move from a twenty-four hour city to one where people go to bed at ten," Drew said. "What do we do? Hitch?"

"No, that's dangerous, even out here. You never know who's driving through." Ray heaved a long sigh and dug out his cell phone. "I'll have to recruit Margaret."

Drew's amusement faded. "Margaret?" Her voice held a strange note.

"Our secretary. Who won't let me hear the end of it, but I'll have to suck it up. Wasn't thinking straight."

His thoughts had all been on Drew. Calling her, hearing her voice, seeing her again, any excuse.

"Hey, Margaret," Ray said as Margaret answered the phone in alarm. "Nah, nothing's wrong. I'm stuck in White Fork and need a ride back to Riverbend. I wouldn't ask you, but I have Drew and Erica with me."

Margaret's expletive exploded through the phone, probably heard all over White Fork. Then she reined in her temper and said, "Be there soon."

Drew was very quiet while they waited. Ray told her and Erica to stay inside the comfortable Lexus while he climbed out to flag Margaret down.

Margaret arrived in a remarkably short time, considering she'd driven from the other side of Riverbend, and totally ignored Ray as she exited her SUV.

"I'm here for your sake, Miss Paresky," she said as Drew and Erica scrambled from the Lexus. "Ray's an idiot."

Drew looked shocked that an employee would speak that way to her employer, but Margaret never kept her opinions to herself. Plus, she'd been hired by Ray's mom and considered she worked for *her*. Ray and Kyle she still viewed as the teenage nuisances who hung around the office.

They settled into Margaret's SUV, Drew in the front, Ray and Erica in the back.

"Can I take you to the B&B?" Margaret asked Drew with great politeness as she pulled onto the highway.

"No—my car's in Riverbend." Drew explained about why they'd brought the Lexus to White Fork. Margaret listened skeptically, casting her eye at Ray in the back seat.

"Huh," Margaret concluded, but she said nothing more about it.

Margaret sped along the straight roads, risking Ross

Campbell's speed traps, but they saw no law enforcement tonight. Or maybe the deputies ran for cover when they saw Margaret behind the wheel.

Margaret dimmed her lights as she pulled up next to Drew's car. "You go on home and get some sleep," Margaret told Drew. "I'll drop Ray off."

"It's no trouble," Drew said quickly. "I can drive him home."

Margaret gave Drew a keen stare as Drew climbed out and half-lifted Erica from the back, Erica sagging against her in exhaustion. Ray slid out as fast as he could, knowing Margaret might simply gun it once Drew and Erica were safe.

Margaret transferred her sharp look to Ray and nodded. "Good night then. See you at the office, Ray."

As soon as Ray shut the back door, Margaret was off, moving swiftly and silently back to the main road.

"I like her," Drew said. "Guess we should get you home."

She gazed at Ray with her sweet blue eyes, her lips parting as though she wanted to say something more.

Erica slid from Drew's arms and crawled tiredly into the back seat of Drew's car, the girl half asleep. Drew's expression turned resigned, and she started up once Ray was buckled in, keeping her lights off until they'd left Dr. Anna's street.

DREW PULLED UP AT RAY'S DARK RANCH HOUSE. SHE HADN'T needed to follow the directions he rumbled, because she'd driven out here before, curiosity leading her.

She hadn't been brave enough that time to turn onto the

drive that led to the ranch house. Now she looked around eagerly, though the darkness hid the bulk of the house. A light illuminated the front porch, the inviting wicker and wooden furniture on it indicating this home was cozy and lived in.

Drew stopped the car and slid out when Ray did. Erica snoozed in the back, the adventure over.

"Thanks," Ray said as Drew quietly closed her door. "I shouldn't have bothered you."

"It was no bother. How will you get to your own truck in the morning?"

Ray shrugged as though leaving his truck parked at the bar was the least of his worries. "I'll have one of the guys drive me in."

"You going to be okay here?" Drew gazed up at the house. While it looked welcoming, it was also silent and empty. Ray would be all alone.

"Sure. Kyle and I tough it out."

He sounded more amused than worried. Of course he didn't worry. This was his home, where he'd been raised, the place where he belonged.

Drew felt a twinge of wistful envy. She'd never had a house of her own, always renting an apartment or someone else's house until her job changed or the rent was raised, forcing her to move to yet another rental. She'd always planned to save for a down payment on a house, however small, but she hadn't ever quite managed it.

The B&B was now her home, for better or worse.

She wanted to ask Ray to come back to it with her, to spend the night. Or for him to invite her in, to find Erica a room to sleep in while she wrapped herself around Ray down the hall.

Too soon, she told herself. And too much to hope for.

Ray stepped to Drew and brushed one knuckle over her cheek. "You go home and get some sleep. Lots of work to do tomorrow."

Drew made herself nod. Work. That's what they had in common, what they clung to. Their excuse to see each other.

Would there be a time they didn't need an excuse?

"Yeah," she said softly. "Good night."

Drew started to turn away, but Ray caught her. His hand was big, callused, strong, but his touch was gentleness itself.

So was the touch on her face, the brush of his fingertips on her lips. Ray leaned closer, his breath on her skin warming.

The kiss, when it came, was the merest touch, as though Ray wanted to learn what only the brush of her lips felt like.

The next kiss was harder, Ray's hand on her back. His mouth was firm but again tender, as though he feared to hurt her.

Drew leaned back on the car, her toes in sneakers digging into the soft earth. Ray came closer, his legs against hers now, the power of his body making hers ache.

A third kiss parted her lips. Drew slid her arms around him, surrendering to the moment. Ray curved over her, his strength amazing, but he didn't frighten her. She felt protected by him, sheltered from the night.

Ray opened her mouth, his tongue moving on hers. Her body reacted, the space between her legs softening and becoming needy. She longed to have his weight on hers in a bed, the hardness she felt in his jeans pressing inside her, opening and completing her.

Drew wanted it so much, she took a sharp breath. She expected Ray to break the kiss, but he tightened his grip on her, slanting his mouth across hers to taste her fully. He made a small sound in his throat, one of need that matched hers.

If they'd been alone, without Erica curled in the back of the car, no glimmer of light from distant trailers where his ranch hands must live, Drew would have wrapped her legs around him, urging him to lift her in his arms, positioning herself directly against him.

She'd kiss the hell out of him and maybe have at him right here, on the hood of her old car. Then drag him into his house and do it again. It had been a long time since Drew had been with a man—years. She figured she'd forgotten how to have sex, but she was willing to relearn with Ray.

His kiss burned. Hands found her waist, her hips, her buttocks. She tasted him, his tongue hard against hers, the muffled groan in his throat sounding in the night.

Ray put his hands on her shoulders and pushed them apart.

They stared at each other, breathing hard. Ray's lips were parted and red, her own tingling and tender.

Ray released her, his fingers curling to his palms. "Guess I better say good night."

Or they'd stand out here kissing until dawn? Drew wished with all her heart they could.

"Yeah." She gave him a smile. "Lots of work." And pasts, and issues, and present difficulties. A new relationship on top of everything might be a little too much.

Or would it? Would being with Ray prove stressful and nerve-wracking, like her marriage to Philip? Or would there be long, slow silences on a Texas evening, and hot leisurely loving all night?

Drew gulped, tamping down these pleasant visions with difficulty. "See you tomorrow."

He hesitated, and she wanted to bite her tongue. Drew's statement assumed Ray had nothing better to do than hang out all day helping put her house back together.

A smile flickered across his face. "See you tomorrow."

Before Drew could do anything foolish, like fling herself into his arms, she opened the car door and got inside.

Ray leaned on the open window as she started the car. He glanced at Erica, oblivious and asleep, and then back at Drew.

"Drive carefully, now."

That was all. But the words were a caress, and might have been the gentlest endearment in the world.

<hr />

THE NEXT MORNING, RAY, HALF-HUNG OVER AND GROGGY, grabbed a ride from one of the ranch hands headed to the feed store. Ray could walk to the bar from there and fetch his truck.

Then he'd go to Drew's. Her parting words—*See you tomorrow*—had made his heart pound, even more than the fantastic kisses she'd given him before that.

She wanted to see him. Figured it was natural for him to arrive at her place in the morning. Like he belonged with her.

No awkwardness, no evasion while each tried to guess what the other wanted, or didn't want. No waiting for her to signal that she'd like him to ask her out, or him signaling that he wanted her to signal him. The strange and fucked-up mating dance.

Instead, she'd simply said, *See you tomorrow*, and the world was right.

When they arrived at Fuller's, Ray spied the gleaming new pickup Blake Haynes had bought for himself. The Hayneses were pains in the ass, had been for years, and Kyle was pretty sure they'd caused Sherrie Duncan's accident.

The moment after Ray spied the truck, he saw Blake and Jarrod Haynes trying to pound the shit out of Kyle.

"Hey, now," the ranch hand, an older guy, called to the tangle as he and Ray boiled from the truck.

Ray knew damn well neither Haynes would listen. He strode rapidly to the fighting mass and plucked Jarrod, the younger brother, away from Kyle. Jarrod struggled until he realized who held him, then he twisted away in panic and ran. Asshole.

Ray moved to take care of Blake, but Blake must have decided two against one weren't his odds. He released Kyle, sent Ray a savage look, and ran after Jarrod, who'd already started Blake's pickup and was screeching away.

Blake's face was bloody—Kyle must have gotten in some good punches. Blake dove into the truck's bed, heaving himself up to yell back at them.

"Still need Ray to save you, Malory. Just like ..." The pickup charged around the corner and was gone.

Ray helped Kyle to his feet. Kyle's face was covered in blood and bruises, and his nice new suit was a mess.

"You okay?" Ray asked in concern. "You look like shit."

Kyle wiped his mouth as Ray steadied him, his hand coming away red.

"He was trying to say 'just like high school,'" Kyle said, voice grating. "And all the times you helped me kick their asses." He grinned, his eyes full of an animated joy that had come from more than just the fight. "Thanks, Ray."

DREW DIDN'T LIKE HOW OFTEN SHE PEERED DOWN THE ROAD that morning, waiting to see a glint of Ray's pickup, or dust rising to announce his arrival. Didn't like how her heart sank when the road remained empty, the sky clear.

Grace Campbell came to pick up Erica right after lunch. Drew had an appointment to enroll and start Erica in school on Monday, and she hoped Erica would be more enthusiastic now that she already had a few friends to go with. She and Grace discussed driving schedules, though most kids took the bus. Erica listened without comment, impatient to get to the ranch and the horses.

Grace also retrieved the pan she'd brought the enchiladas in, washed and cleaned by Drew. Drew waved Erica and Grace off, and emptiness settled on the B&B.

Drew continued with her painting, but when she caught sight of the photos of her grandparents Erica had propped on a shelf, she took a break and studied them again.

Her grandfather and grandmother leaned on the porch, smiling in confidence. They'd been so young, so full of optimism.

Drew remembered her grandmother only as an elderly woman, seemingly happy with her children and grandchildren. She'd never remarried, but had many friends of both genders.

Erica was much like her, everyone said, outgoing and gregarious. The woman in the photo showed the resemblance.

Had Drew's grandfather loved her grandmother so much he couldn't let go of this place once she'd gone? Too many memories of her? No matter how far it went to ruin?

Drew would like to talk to Mrs. Kaye again, and others who might have known her grandparents. There must be a reason her grandfather had stipulated that Drew keep the property and restore it.

She growled and threw down the photos.

"Something wrong?"

"Ray!" Drew had never been so happy to hear a rumbling voice. She took a few steps toward him but checked herself. Dignity. She still had that. Right?

"Sorry I'm so late," Ray said. "Had to take my brother to the clinic."

Drew halted in concern. "Is he all right?"

Ray looked unworried. "He is. Got his ass kicked a little bit by the town bullies, but nothing broke. He's home recovering."

Drew blinked. For some reason she imagined she'd leave violence behind in the big city, but people lost their tempers everywhere, she supposed. She hoped Kyle was okay.

"Did he say how it went with Dr. Anna?" she asked, thinking of the Lexus in front of the dark house. "None of my business ... No, to heck with that. I want to know."

"He was still wearing his suit this morning and got in the fight because one of the bullies badmouthed Anna." Ray rubbed his chin, as though thinking about it. "I'd say it's going okay."

Drew shared his smile. "I wish them well."

"I wish they'd get on with it. Anna's house is small, so they'd be better off living at the ranch, and it wouldn't be so quiet."

"So easy to solve everyone else's problems," Drew said with a little sigh.

"Yep."

Because emotions didn't get in the way when Drew wasn't directly affected. They clouded and confused when the problem was her own.

The philosophical question was interrupted by Drew's phone. Erica. "Hi, honey. Everything okay?"

"Everything's wonderful. Faith wants me to spend the night, and Grace and Olivia say it's all right. Please, Mom? *Pleeeeze?*"

"Of course it's all right." Drew had never been this confident leaving Erica with anyone before, but Grace Campbell was an angel. "Remember not to be a nuisance, and help clean up."

"I know all that stuff. Tell Ray hi. Is he there?"

"He is now."

"Hi, Ray!" Erica yelled, and Drew painfully lifted the phone from her ear. Ray grinned. "See you, Mom. Thank you. Love you so much."

"Love you too, honey."

Erica had already hung up. Drew laid down the phone, and then her amusement died.

"It's always so quiet when she isn't here. Not sure how I'll get through a night by myself."

She rubbed her arms, glancing out the window at the long, endless stretch of green.

Ray was next to her, his warmth easing her sudden chill. "I can stay with you. In fact, I'd rather. I don't like the thought of you out here alone."

Chapter Ten

Ray waited for Drew to withdraw, throw him out. He knew she hadn't been hinting for him to stay—her confession of loneliness had come from the heart.

Wasn't anything for Ray to go home to either. Kyle was pissed off at the Hayenses and uncertain about Anna, which made him growly and short-tempered. Ray would take the peace and quiet of Drew's place anytime.

Drew gave him a quick nod. "Okay." Her smile returned. "You'll need a toothbrush."

"I'll run into town later and grab a few things."

Drew looked grateful and then worried. They were both feeling their way.

"I'll get back to work on the porch," Ray said. "After I snag me one of these." He snatched up one of the cupcakes Grace had brought when she'd picked up Erica, and took a huge bite. It was yellow cake with girly pink frosting, but Ray didn't care. Grace's cupcakes tasted good no matter what they looked like.

Drew regarded him with merriment. "You have frosting on your face."

Ray shrugged, loving the light in Drew's eyes. He couldn't answer with his mouth full of cake.

He grabbed his tools and headed downstairs before he could do anything stupid like smear the frosting on Drew so he could have the pleasure of licking it off.

DREW DECIDED TO COOK. IF RAY WAS STAYING OVER, SHE could be hospitable and fix him a meal.

She'd like to wow him with Chicago-style Italian food, best pizza in the world, but she didn't know where to get the ingredients. Not that it was tomato season anyway.

From what she'd seen since arriving, Riverbenders liked barbecued anything and Tex-Mex. Drew didn't have a grill, so she decided on Tex-Mex. She'd seen plenty of ingredients for that at the local grocery.

While Ray worked, she went shopping, bought what the woman who ran the grocery store advised, and brought the food home. He disappeared to town himself after she returned, probably to pick up his things for the overnight.

Drew's awareness thrummed as she worked, sorting the groceries and deciding on a recipe. Nothing too complicated but something more than simply stuffing meat into a taco shell.

Ray returned as she was contemplating the mysteries of chile peppers.

"The grocer told me these were better for seasoning than chili powders." Drew sorted the peppers by size—a large, elongated dark green one, a narrower, lighter green one, and a small dark green one. "But I don't know which is which, or what is hot and what isn't. At home, when I made Mexican food, I used powdered seasoning from a packet."

Ray set down a backpack on one of the cracked barstools they'd found in the garage. "We use packets too. She's messing with you. I bet you asked her how to make it authentic."

Drew had to nod. "She was so helpful."

"Huh. I'm sure. *That* is a poblano." He pointed to the largest pepper, dark green and fresh-looking. "Those are fairly mild. This one's a jalapeño." His finger went to the small dark green one. "A little bit hotter—you've probably heard of them."

Drew's brow puckered. "I've only had them batter fried or chopped up on nachos. They look different right off the plant."

"This one's a serrano." Ray indicated the long, thin pepper. "Hottest of what you have here. There are hotter ones out there, but serrano has a nice bite. You can tone down the heat, if you want—take out all the ribs and seeds when you cut it up."

"Which I have no idea how to do." Drew took out the chef's knife she'd brought carefully from home and stared at it, then the chiles.

"Let me wash up, and I'll show you." Ray grabbed his pack and disappeared to the bathroom.

Drew's heart beat faster. She hadn't had a man stay over for a long time, and the occurrence had been rare, in any case. She hadn't wanted to bring someone home for sex with Erica sleeping in the next room—or not sleeping, which would be more likely. She and her guy of the moment had usually gone off on a weekend together, while Erica stayed behind with a babysitter. Drew hadn't been comfortable with that solution either.

Ray was different. She didn't feel weird bringing him into the house—not that this was much of a house—and Erica liked him. In fact, Erica liked him so much Drew worried how upset her daughter would be if things between Ray and Drew didn't work out.

Erica had been very young when Drew and Philip had separated and didn't remember much about him. She'd envied other kids who'd had real dads, though she'd never complained much. She'd understood about life and death at a too early age.

If Erica grew attached to Ray, and Drew and Ray broke up …

Jumping the gun, Ray had said. He'd been speaking about Kyle and Anna, but the advice was as relevant to Ray and Drew.

She should concentrate on the now, not on the what might be. Take things as they came. It was how she'd survived her darkest days.

Ray returned from the bathroom, sleeves of his shirt rolled up to reveal tanned forearms creased with tiny white scars. He rummaged in a cupboard for a bowl, which he set next to the chopping board. Drew couldn't take her eyes off him. Easy to tell herself she'd take things slow with him when he wasn't right next to her, his hard body sending her libido soaring.

"You cut 'em up like bell peppers," Ray said as he sliced the serrano neatly down the middle. He pulled it apart and used the knife to take out the core of seeds and then to skim out the ribs.

He did it competently, easily, like it was nothing. He

handed Drew the knife and turned to wash his hands in the sink.

"Try the poblano," he said over his shoulder. "It's big and easier to cut. Don't get too many of the juices on your hands, though. Those peppers are milder but they can still sting."

Drew cut open the pepper to find it indeed looked much like a red or green bell pepper inside, just a different shape. Once she took out the seeds, Ray showed her how to slide the knife under the ribs to slice them away and drop them into a slop bowl.

Drew was confident enough after cutting up the poblanos to do the few jalapeños. Smaller, but same principle.

"Do you always take out the ribs and seeds? To make them more mild?"

"Kyle chops them up whole and throws them into the chili pot. But …" Ray trailed off, cheekbones reddening.

"But I'm a wimpy northerner?" Drew narrowed her eyes. "I'll have you know we eat pretty hot stuff in Chicago, buddy. How do you think we get through the cold winters?"

Ray grinned. "You're a Texan by blood. That never leaves you. But yeah, I'm introducing you to southwestern chiles a little bit at a time."

"And I'm grateful." Drew set to chopping. "I don't need my mouth on fire."

Ray's answering look made everything in her tingle. Another guy might follow up with a sexy witticism about her fiery mouth, but Ray wasn't a man of overly clever sayings and constant jokes. He said what he needed to, and then he shut up.

Drew found it restful. She never felt forced to keep up with his banter, wondering what he'd say next and how she should react.

When Ray did speak, he carried on a normal conversation. Nothing demanding, no challenging her to return the repartee or be derided if she couldn't.

Ray went through the recipe the woman at the grocery store had given her, and they cooked it together. He showing her how to sear the peppers and then the meat, then let the mess of it plus some garlic and onion cook together until the sauce was tender and juicy. It smelled wonderful.

Drew ducked into the bathroom while the meat and peppers simmered. When she emerged again, she approached Ray hesitantly.

"Um ..."

Ray turned around. He'd taken out the package of flour tortillas they'd roll the meat in to make burritos. "You okay?" he asked in concern.

"I ... uh ..." Drew's face heated until it burned like the rest of her. "I think I didn't wash the pepper juice off my hands well enough before I used the bathroom." She felt her flush deepen. "I'm tingling in the wrong places."

Ray stared at her for a long moment. Philip would have immediately told her she was careless or plain stupid and have no sympathy. Ray regarded her blankly, as though trying to decide how to react.

Then he dropped the package of tortillas on the counter with a splat, folded his arms over his gut, and laughed. Loud, long uproarious laughter she'd never heard from him before. He'd given a chuckle here and there, even a guffaw, but not this belly-hard, deep from within himself laughter.

Drew fell into laughter with him. Just watching him holding his sides, face creased, eyes squeezed closed, made her life better.

"It's not funny," she gasped. "I might have done myself some serious damage."

Ray opened his eyes, sparkling and green, and dragged in a long breath. "We'd better get you cleaned up then." He took her arm and steered her the short way to the bathroom. His laughter had abated somewhat but still shook him all over.

Drew realized what he meant when he skimmed back the shower curtain and turned on the water. His hands went to her shirt to slide it up and off, and she froze.

Ray stilled as well. His eyes asked the question.

She wanted him. Drew knew that with every beat of her heart. But accepting what he silently offered would take her into the realm of no return. Kissing him was one thing. Surrendering to her desires was something else.

Ray caressed her waist, his hand strong. He was a big man, but he gentled his touch, making it her decision.

Drew could stop this now, send him away ... and be a little less than she had been before she'd met him. He'd given her kindness, friendship, caring, help when she needed it. When he left, a part of her would go with him.

Drew moved his hands quietly aside but before he could register hurt or resignation, she slid her shirt off over her head and popped the button on her shorts.

Chapter Eleven

❧❦❧

Ray's breath stopped. Drew had been laughing so hard tears had leaked from her eyes. The harsh glare of the bathroom light glittered on those tears now, soft on her cheeks.

Her belly came into view, a little rounded, scarred from carrying a child. Her breasts, plump and full, were heavy in a pink lacy bra. The bra was a touch of the feminine among her paint-splotched work clothes.

She'd slid open the button of her shorts, fingers hesitating. Ray reached for the zipper and glided it down.

Drew took a sharp breath. Ray kept going, hands seeking her warmth encased in satin. He found himself kissing her, the natural thing to do while he slid down the shorts, slipping fingers beneath the waistband of her panties.

Drew tugged at his shirt, dislodging buttons. It was an old shirt that had seen better riding days, and the loosened fabric fell easily from Ray's shoulders.

He dropped the shirt and returned to Drew to slide her underwear down, her skin as silken as the panties. He found her heat waiting for him, liquid and pooling. Drew's kisses turned deep, she clutching at Ray to draw him closer.

But chile juices could burn and blister, and while he'd laughed at her, Ray also knew they had to wash it off her. He left off the kissing to unhook her bra and then lift her into the shower.

Ray let his gaze rove her bared body, her nipples tightening under his gaze. Water beaded on Drew's skin and dripped from her hair, turning it dark as midnight.

He reached past her for the pale bottle of liquid soap on the tub's lip, squirted a large amount on his hands, lathered her skin.

Ray's breath came fast as he wiped her body with the soap, her skin slippery and pliant, and his cock rose, hard and tight. Drew went motionless, her eyes half closing in pleasure, letting Ray wash her.

He massaged and caressed the soap all over her. Best was rubbing it on her breasts, her nipples dark in the middle of soft flesh. He caught her nipples between his fingers, gently playing.

He slid the soap down across her belly to tickle her belly button, then between her legs, washing away what stung.

Drew stilled. The bathtub's bottom sat a few inches above the floor, which meant Drew only had to tilt her head back a little to meet Ray's gaze. Her eyes were filled with hunger, a desire as hot as the steam rising around them.

One of Ray's fingers slipped inside her. Drew gasped, then she put her hand on his shoulder, grip biting down.

Ray played his finger inside her incredible heat, letting his palm rub her opening, bringing her to life.

Drew's eyes drifted closed, and she groaned. She shuddered, skin prickling with goosebumps despite the hot water streaming over her. She lifted her face to the shower, letting it rain on her while she rocked on Ray's hand.

Ray wanted to rip off his jeans, leap into the tub with her, and have her against the wall, but he held off. She needed this pleasure to be all her own. Her quick reaction to him, the tightening of her muscles around his finger, told him it had been a while. She was going to release, and quickly.

He was halfway under the falling water, his arm around her, lips on hers, when she did come. She did it beautifully, moving against him hard and fast, a cry of pure joy escaping her lips.

She cried out, loud in the small room, then her laughter rolled over him. Drew collapsed against the wall, still laughing.

Ray quickly divested himself of the rest of his clothes and climbed under the shower with her.

"I'm already wet," he said, kissing her face, her lips. "Might as well."

Wet and slippery, Drew pulled Ray to her, kissing him as she sealed them together. They kissed for a long time, tasting, licking, learning, nibbling, until Drew snatched up the bottle of body wash.

Ray got in a, "Hey now," before she squirted it all over him. She followed that with her hands, lathering him up.

She smoothed soap over his chest, playing with *his* nipples, which tingled like bites of fire. Around to his back, sweetly soothing, then down to his cock.

Ray started as she closed her hand around him, soap making everything slick. He froze as she slid her hand up his hard cock, squeezing just right.

It had been a long time for him too. The buckle bunnies who'd chased Ray and Kyle had been eager and willing, and

Ray had enjoyed them some years back. But these days he wanted more. He wanted someone to *be* with, to share his good times and hug him during the bad, to talk with, to be quiet with. Not a woman who simply wanted to be with a champion bull rider. The women who'd followed him on the rodeo circuit had wanted Ray's body, not his pain.

Drew hadn't once asked about his bull riding. She never asked him about how many trophies he'd won or how much prize money he'd had, or how many sponsorships he'd been offered. She didn't judge him on any of that. She just accepted him as he was.

Because of all this, plus not having had sex for longer than he cared to think about, Ray came fast and hard as Drew stroked him, right into her hand.

Drew looked delighted. She let the shower clean them off while she stepped into Ray's arms, holding him while they caressed and kissed, coming down from their release.

Ray needed more. He reached around Drew and shut off the water, then he carried her, both of them dripping wet, to her bedroom.

It was a tiny chamber, big enough for a bed and not much else, but a bed was all they needed. Ray stretched on top of Drew in the sunshine, she gazing up at him with soft eyes.

The heat from the late afternoon sun dried them and added to their languidness, but it couldn't calm the fervor that had begun inside him. He wanted this woman, needed her.

Ray had left his backpack in the bathroom, so he'd been able to grab from it what he wanted on the way to the bedroom. When he'd gone home to fetch his toothbrush earlier today, he'd picked up some condoms, just in case.

He reached for one now, grinning a little at Drew's look

of approval. He opened it, and she helped him slide it on without embarrassment, Ray so hard his cock was flushed and dark.

Tossing aside the wrapper, he rolled Drew onto the mattress, looking into her beautiful blue eyes as he slid inside her.

This was all he needed. Wonderful Drew, the sunshine, and being in her. Ray let out a groan as he started loving her, something within him finally awakening.

———

RAY WAS A SLOW LOVER, DREW CAME TO KNOW AS SHE LOST herself in him. His strength was incredible, as was his unhurried touch.

He was also a fast and powerful lover, she learned as well. As his thrusts built, his leisurely calm fell away, until they were driving at each other, cries and shouts echoing. They were alone, a long way from any neighbors, and they could be as loud as they liked.

It was freeing, lying in this nest with Ray, Drew pouring forth everything pent up within her.

Ray kissed her, loved her hard, reaching between them to caress and stroke her.

At the end, they were both crying each other's names, moving fast, frantic, sweat-streaked, and still wet from the shower. A wave of pure pleasure rolled under Drew and swept her up, spinning her around with this beautiful man, who cradled her in safety.

They landed, washed up on the shore that was the mattress while the waves of their passion ebbed. Ray looked down at her, his granite-hard face relaxed from his release, afterglow kisses brushing her skin.

Drew held Ray close, and they lay together in silence, while dusk fell, coating the room in easy darkness.

———

DREW BIT INTO THE SAVORY PILLOW OF THE BURRITO, THE filling having simmered to perfection while she'd been enjoying herself with Ray. She glanced at Ray across the uneven table, and he looked at her at the same time.

His lazy smile undid her. Drew wanted to leap across the table, snuggle into his lap, and kiss him silly.

"These turned out well," she said, trying to keep her thoughts corralled.

"Whole day turned out well."

Drew flushed. "Yeah, it did."

Ray glanced at the freshly painted walls and sanded floorboards. "We've made some progress."

"Yeah," Drew said. "We have."

Ray reached over and took her hand. They'd moved from awkward friends to easy intimacy, which was both relaxing and exciting. Drew was supposed to be wary, concerned about where this was going now that they'd made love, but those worries didn't come.

"Like I mentioned before, I don't like the idea of you staying out here alone," Ray said after another time of silence. "You'll start getting in building materials, and that will make you a target for thieves—even River County has them."

"I could get a guard dog," Drew said. "Cinders isn't much of a guard cat." The half-grown Cinders liked everyone.

Ray let his lips quirk in appreciation of her humor. "I was thinking I'd stay here. Not just tonight. I could sleep on the couch."

Because Erica might not like it if Ray suddenly started sleeping in Drew's bed. Sweet of him to think about that.

"Couch is too small for you," Drew pointed out. "Not to mention saggy and hard."

"There's a couple of sofas lying around my house no one is using." Ray studied Drew over the beer bottle he'd lifted. "Seriously, it's not safe for you to be out here alone."

He didn't ask her opinion or permission, just decided she needed him to be there for her. Drew liked that.

She also liked that he didn't act as though Drew was stupid for not thinking of it herself. He saw a problem and he offered a solution.

Drew slid her bare foot across to him and up the leg of his jeans. "I'm sure we can work it out."

Ray set down the beer, a smile on his lips. He rose and came to her, lifting Drew out of her chair to sit in it himself and have her straddle him. He took her face in his hands and kissed her, thoroughly and heatedly.

Dinner could wait.

RAY SLEPT WITH DREW THAT NIGHT. WHEN HE WOKE IN morning sunshine, her legs entwined with his, a lightness settled on his heart.

They cooked breakfast together, elbows and hips bumping, and kissed long and leisurely before they finally ate the cooling eggs and hash browns.

He left when she drove to the Campbells to pick up Erica.

He needed to go home and grab some more things if he'd make his move here longer term.

They locked up everything, and shared another deep kiss before Ray watched Drew drive away in her little car.

She'd need to do something about the car as well. A truck would be a lot more practical for her. Ray would have to help her shop for one—maybe the grant money the Campbells were sure to give her would cover a vehicle.

As he drove, he noted that the world was a bit brighter, shinier. Had the Clifton ranch's fence ever looked so clean, like a white light leading down the highway? Had the town square always been so full of blooming flowers, the couples with picnic baskets so contented, their kids so wild and happy?

Probably, but Ray hadn't noticed before. Or maybe he was coating everything with a joy that had been absent until last night, when Drew had lain his arms.

No, that was too poetic for what they'd done. They'd grappled with each other, having hot, hard, and mind-blowing sex. The best sex of his life.

Ray was whistling when he drove onto his ranch, the sun shining, the sky brilliantly blue, puffy clouds extra puffy. The house, three stories of home, gray-white with green shutters —Grace's and Lucy's choice—opened its arms and welcomed him.

Dr. Anna's truck with shoeing trailer was parked between office and house, but he didn't see her around. Ray, hungry now, strolled inside and to the kitchen, ready to fix himself a big sandwich before he started packing up to stay at Drew's.

The house was quiet, peaceful—until Ray heard the long groan drifting from upstairs.

He peered up the staircase in alarm, wondering if Kyle

had fallen and hurt himself, but then he halted, mirth rising as he recognized exactly what he was hearing. Kyle's gruff voice sounded from his room high under the eaves, blending with female answering cries.

Ray stifled laughter. *Finally.* He crept back to the kitchen, shutting the door to muffle the noises. He'd make a sandwich and take it to the office. He needed to explain to Margaret that he was moving to Drew's for a while, and she'd have to contact him there.

Everything had gone quiet by the time he'd taken out lunch meat and mustard and other stuff and started building a giant sandwich. Footsteps sounded on the stairs. The door burst open behind him, and Anna's and Kyle's secret laughter sputtered to a halt.

"Ray," Kyle said in shock when Ray turned around. "What are you doing here?"

"I live here." Ray transferred his gaze to Anna, noting a smear of what looked like chocolate on her cheek. "I take it you're done upstairs? Good, because I want to have lunch."

Anna flushed until she was brick-colored, and Ray took pity on her and looked away.

"Don't worry, I'm outta here," Anna said rapidly. "Have an office to get back to."

"Better swing home and wash up," Ray said as he continued with his sandwich. "So no one thinks you were mud wrestling."

"Fuck you, Ray," Kyle growled.

Ray looked around in surprise at Kyle's vehemence. "I'm not trying to be an asshole. Just save her some embarrassment."

"No, he's right," Anna said. "Everyone's already talking enough. See you, Kyle."

She charged out the back door, the windows rattling from the door's slam, and strode determinedly to her truck.

Ray motioned after her with his water bottle. "Better walk her out, or she might never come back."

Kyle glared at him, snarled *Shit*, and raced out after Anna. Ray watched as Kyle caught up to her, their momentary awkwardness dissolving. Kyle touched Anna's cheek, and Ray returned to making his sandwich, glad for them, and for himself.

LATER, RAY PACKED UP A BAG AND A BOX AND RETURNED TO the B&B, every movement feeling effortless. When he rolled onto the dirt lot in front of the garage, he found Karen Marvin's BMW already parked there.

Hoping she'd come with good news about the grant, Ray left the bag and box in the truck and hurried up the stairs. No need to broadcast to Karen that he was moving in.

Karen sat on a barstool, her long legs crossed. Drew stood in the middle of the room, more anger in her eyes than Ray had ever seen.

"Drew." Ray moved to her and put his hands on her shoulders. "You all right, baby?"

"No." Drew's voice was hard, but she didn't pull away or look embarrassed at the endearment. "I'm not all right. And neither is my brother-in-law. He's trying to take everything away from me."

Chapter Twelve

D rew spun away from Ray, who stood like a sturdy pillar, and blinked to keep the tears back.

"Tell me what happened," Ray growled at Karen.

Karen faced him, her cool eyes filled with anger. "Her dickhead brother-in-law—do you mind if I call him a dickhead, Drew? Her dickhead brother-in-law called AGCT and tried to get us to drop the grant. I don't know a) how he knew about it, and b) why he thought I'd listen to him."

"Drop it? Why?"

Karen shrugged. "Said Drew was incompetent and more likely to abscond with the funding than use it for the B&B."

"What'd you tell him?" Ray's face set in a scowl.

"I thanked him for his call and said I'd take his opinion into consideration. Which I have. Don't worry, Drew, I consider his opinion utter bullshit."

Drew relaxed a fraction. "Why should you? You don't know me. He could be right."

"Please, honey. This isn't my first rodeo. Or my second, or my third. He doesn't understand that one) I do my

research thoroughly and two) this is a small town." Karen
liked to put things into neat categories. "I'm not a faceless
woman behind a desk perusing your paperwork. I meet
people, talk to them. Know where they live, know their
kids, and who they date." She finished with a pointed look
at Ray.

"Drew's a good risk," Ray said. "You have *my* word
on that."

"I know." Karen flashed irritation. "I didn't come over to
say I'd turned down the grant on the word of an asshole. I
came to warn her. This guy sounds like trouble."

"He is." Drew sank to the sofa, her legs too shaky to let
her stand. "He blames me for my husband's death, thinks I
can't take care of Erica, and did *not* want me to move to
Riverbend and save the B&B. He hired a lawyer to try to
prevent me taking Erica out of the state, but since I'm her
legal guardian and Jules isn't—not even close—he couldn't
make it fly."

Karen studied her in puzzlement. "Why would he want to
block you fixing up the B&B? If you do, you get the rest of
the money. You could take care of Erica just fine then, and if
this Jules dickhead is sweet to you, you might share some of
that payout."

"I don't know." Drew heaved a sigh. "I made those same
points to him when we argued about it. Jules told me I was
incompetent at everything and might as well quit before I
start." She balled her fists. "*He* is one of the reasons I made
the decision to come here. I wanted to take up the challenge,
show him he was wrong."

Ray came to her. Regardless of Karen sitting on the
barstool watching every move, he sat next to Drew and put
his arm around her.

"And you *will* show him," he said, his voice rumbling. "I swear that. I'm helping you, Karen is helping—we all are."

That was true. Since Drew had arrived in Riverbend, she'd been mostly embraced. She'd believed she'd be shunned as an outsider, but people had been friendly and interested from the start.

"Thank you," she said softly. "But Jules worries me. He has powerful friends. He tried very hard to take Erica away from me after Philip died, saying I'd never be able to raise her on my own."

"Obviously, you won that fight," Karen pointed out. "And you'll win this one." She frowned, her perfect face crinkling the slightest bit. "What I don't understand is how he knew. At AGCT, we don't announce who we're funding until we hand over the check."

"Erica." Drew knew this in her heart. "She talks to Jules all the time. He's nice to her, and she likes him—she doesn't understand what a snake he can be. She'll find out sooner or later, but I'm trying not to take away everyone in her life."

"Commendable," Karen said. "But I think it's time to cut that tie. You were trying to give her a father figure, probably out of guilt. Women love guilt, don't we? Which is why I gave it up a long time ago. But now Erica has Ray to be her father figure, so you can tell her the truth about Uncle Jules."

Karen's blunt statements hit Drew like blows, though she agreed with every single one.

She turned to see what Ray thought about being called Erica's new father figure, but he was nodding slowly. "You sure don't need a guy like that in your life."

"Definitely not." Karen continued arranging Drew's world for her. "When I was young, I was very pretty, so of course all the men lined up to go to bed with me—and then tell me what to do with my life afterward, in detail. Because of course I'd never be able to think for myself. After I split with my second husband, I decided I'd had enough of men bullying me. I went all out for my career, and had men on the side for fun. Works a dream, I have to tell you."

Drew flushed, but Ray didn't look embarrassed at Karen's frankness.

"Don't worry about your brother-in-law," he said to Drew. "There's nothing he can do legally. Right?" he asked Karen.

"He can't block the grant," Karen answered. "That is entirely the purview of AGCT Enterprises. The Campbells like you, Drew, and already adore Erica, so no problem there. Jules shouldn't be able to block your grandfather's trust or its stipulations either. That's *your* side of the family, not his."

"He's been a pain in my ass since the day I married Philip," Drew said, old anger stirring. "I was never good enough for his baby brother."

"Family." Karen made a dismissive gesture then hopped off the stool and straightened her skirt. "I ditched mine and have been much happier since. Not that you have to worry about Ray's family. Grace loves you already, and Kyle is reasonable about everything but Dr. Anna." She brightened. "Did I tell you I saw them at Chez Orleans? Making googly eyes at each other. It was so cute."

She beamed them a big smile then said goodbye and let herself out. Drew walked with her to the stairs, thanking her.

"No problem, honey. You needed to know. But don't worry too much and enjoy yourself." She glanced pointedly back at Ray, winked at Drew, then marched briskly down the stairs, her good deed done. In a moment, Drew heard the purr of her car as she started the engine.

Drew returned to the apartment, wandering to the window to watch her drive away. "I'm sorry about that."

"What for?" Ray came up behind her, his arms going around her. "Not your fault. Karen's right about letting go of guilt. It messes you up—trust me, I've had my share."

"Sorry to drag you into my problems," Drew clarified. "Sorry my husband's brother is such an asshole, and that Karen assumes you're fine with solving all my issues."

Ray kissed her cheek, his breath warm. "Karen isn't wrong." He huffed a laugh. "She's full of shit, though. She says she's done with family, but she's made Riverbend her family. She's as gossipy and interfering as anyone around. She'll be just like Mrs. Kaye when she's older."

Drew had to smile at that. "Think she'll still be dating young cowboys then?"

"Who knows? Though I think she's getting tired of Deke and looking to move on. She wasn't happy with him the other night."

Drew turned in his arms, liking his solidness behind her. Her smile faded. "Jules won't give up. He's been badgering me for years."

"Doesn't matter." Ray kissed her, sending fires through her blood. "We'll deal with him. And you will fix this place up and show him what you can do."

When Ray said it, she believed it.

She also wanted to keep kissing him, so she rose on tiptoes and pressed a slow burning kiss to his mouth.

Erica had begged to stay longer at the Campbells earlier this morning, and Drew had agreed. Which meant she and Ray were alone in the cozy apartment, and the bed waited in a pool of sunshine.

LUCY MALORY LET HER CAR IDLE ON THE LAST HILL ABOVE THE Malory ranch, her home spreading before her.

Two days ago, she'd stood with her coworkers at a glitzy party in a glitzy hotel ballroom, drinking champagne and waiting for Clyde Gordon, her boss and boyfriend, to make his announcement. The company had done well this year, so maybe he would proclaim huge bonuses for all, more even than last year. Clyde hadn't told Lucy what the announcement was, so she had no answer for her friends, no matter how much they bugged her.

She recalled exactly how the champagne flute had felt in her hand, the smooth, cold hardness of the glass, made a bit slippery with tiny beads of condensation, the soft sound of the bubbles, the lingering taste of the champagne's sweetness in her mouth.

Exactly how one strap of her gown had pressed on her shoulder and how one shoe had felt a little tight as Clyde had stepped up on the stage at the end of the ballroom. A young woman Lucy had seen vaguely around the office building in the last week had gone up to stand next to him.

Clyde raised his glass and called out, "Join me in congratulating the future Mrs. Gordon!"

For a split second, Lucy had thought Clyde was talking about her. She remembered her spike of joy and surprise—he'd said nothing to her about this.

She'd nearly started running for the stage, before ice-cold, knifelike realization struck her. He meant he was marrying the beautiful, svelte, and radiant woman beside him. He took the woman's hand and raised it high.

The crowd had quieted in amazement, then they'd

cheered. Amid the tumult, Lucy had fled the room and the hotel, barely able to see.

After a night of pacing in her apartment, alternately crying and cursing, avoiding the phone and texted questions of her friends, Lucy had confronted Clyde in his office, blowing past his PA, who'd tried to keep her out.

The man with sexy blue eyes, who'd given her smoldering smiles and spent weekends in South Padre Island with her drinking margaritas and making love, regarded her now in cold blankness.

Who he married was his business, he said. He and Lucy'd had fun, but …

Lucy, who was no man's doormat, told him exactly what she thought. Clyde only gazed at her as though bored and said, "Clear out your desk, Luce. You're done."

Numb, she'd carefully placed all her personal items from her office into a cardboard file box and marched out as everyone on her floor watched. Security guards waited at the elevator to escort her. When she told them hotly there was no need for that, they only gave her bland stares and accompanied her all the way to her car. They even stood and watched while she started up and drove off—*after* she relinquished her keycard to the garage.

Not that Lucy would ever dream of setting foot in this building or even driving down the street it lay on ever again.

She went straight to her apartment, which fortunately, she paid for herself, dumped her office trinkets, including the photo of her and Clyde feeding each other oysters at a fancy banquet, and stuffed clothes haphazardly into an overnight bag.

No wonder Clyde had never acted on her hints that she move in with him, since Lucy spent so much time at his house anyway. No wonder, after their last weekend together at a quiet B&B in Marfa, he'd said he'd be preparing hard for end-of-quarter reports and Lucy should stay at her own place for a while. Didn't want to bore her out of her mind, Clyde had said.

He'd been preparing all right, to marry the daughter of his father's old business partner and drop the bombshell at the company's next party.

Lucy, in her anguish, could think of only one place to go. Only one place in the world where she could withdraw and lick her wounds. She'd driven straight from her apartment and through the endless city, out across the state on the I-10, and then down smaller highways to the calm familiarity of Riverbend.

Not until she paused at this hill and saw home waiting for her, beckoning her on, did she balk. Her brothers and sister would want to know why she'd come home and what had happened, and she'd be plunged into humiliation.

She *could* flee somewhere no one knew her, blow all her money on a month-long cruise to the Caribbean where she could meet another single and have mindless, tequila-soaked sex.

Which had the potential to end in disaster. Besides, the sight of the Malory ranch had loosened all the tightness inside her.

Lucy put her car in gear and rolled down the hill and through the gates. She didn't want to see anyone, but there was Margaret, heading out of the office on her ruthless surveillance of the ranch.

Margaret halted in surprise when she saw Lucy climb from her car, then her face softened in concern. "Lucy? You all right?"

Good old Margaret, solid, strong, taking no shit. She'd have put Clyde in his place. Lucy wanted to laugh, thinking about it, but if she did, she'd probably start bawling.

Lucy pasted on a false smile, her eyes stinging. "Decided to come home for a while. Kyle or Ray around?"

"No, they're …"

Lucy didn't wait for her to finish. If Kyle and Ray were out, the house would be refreshingly empty. She hurried toward it, tears flooding as she ran up the porch to her embracing home, the place of her childhood—her dreams, her hopes, her youthful happiness.

She made it to the living room and the sofa before she had to fall on it and give herself over to weeping.

Kyle found her there. Lucy realized, as Kyle held her after she sobbed out the story, how much she loved her brother, and what that love truly meant to her.

AT THE BAR THAT EVENING, RAY WATCHED HIS SISTER AND Kyle stand side-by-side while Lucy faced down the town. He was proud of her, holding her head up and smiling at the curious Riverbenders.

If Ray ever came across that Clyde asshole, he'd grind the man's face into the nearest wall. Kyle agreed with him. But Lucy had a home here, no questions, no judgment.

So did Drew. Karen and AGCT Enterprises had come through today, three days after Karen's last visit, Karen stopping by to present Drew a check. Ray had gone into town with Drew to deposit it in her business account, then they'd gone to Fuller's, placing a huge order for supplies, and also with Jack's contracting business.

They'd celebrated at home with Erica and more of Grace's cupcakes. Then Kyle had called Ray about Lucy, and Ray had gone home to help comfort her.

Hal Jenkins, a former bull rider turned rodeo clown, entered from where he'd been hanging out with Jack on the porch. Hal was a slow-speaking, solid man, who'd grown tired of falling off bulls and decided to help bull riders stay safe in the ring instead.

Hal sat down at the end of the bar near Ray, but his gaze was on Lucy. He didn't try to elbow into the group around her or join the conversation, but Hal watched her. *Hmm.*

Kyle had told Ray about cattle being stolen from the ranch Hal managed. Turned out Malory cattle had gone missing as well. People truly sucked.

Ray sat back and watched Lucy try to be strong, and Hal watching Lucy. Hal was a good guy, one Ray wouldn't mind hanging out with his sister, but Lucy probably wasn't in the mood for good guys right now—any guys.

Dr. Anna watched the group too, but her gaze was on Kyle. She'd make a great sister-in-law and addition to the family. Ray looked forward to it.

Anna turned to speak to Tina, a rodeo groupie who was really a nice kid. Ray saw Anna's expression grow concerned, then she went straight to Kyle. Something bad was up.

Ray rose to see what, Hal coming with him. "Anna thinks she might know where the rustled cattle are," Kyle said, his face alive with excitement. "Help us find out?"

Kyle had a new energy, the pain of his injuries forgotten. Probably for the same reason Ray was finding renewed interest in life. A beautiful woman did that.

"Let's go," Ray said.

Hal set down his beer, ready to help, but sent a regretful glance at Lucy.

Ray called Drew, explaining the situation and telling her he might be late getting back.

Ray reflected, as he followed his brother and Hal out, that it was nice he had someone to call, someone to say to him in her soft voice, "Be careful."

EVERYTHING SHOULD HAVE BEEN FINE, DREW THOUGHT IN rage the next morning.

Should have been going great. Drew now had grant money to help her with the massive renovations of the house. The growing intimacy between her and Ray made her heart sing. Erica had attended her first day of school and come home excited and happy, begging her mom to sign release forms so she could join band, the softball team, and the horseback riding club.

Their lives should now be smooth and sweet, reward within Drew's grasp.

But in the typical way of things, it suddenly started to go wrong.

It began the morning after Ray had helped locate the stolen cattle—Drew was amazed that cattle rustling was still a thing. Drew woke to find the porch floor of the main house, the one Ray had spent a week painstakingly replacing, entirely torn up, the new boards scattered over the grass, broken and ruined.

Chapter Thirteen

✦

Drew stood amid the ruined boards, hands on hips, her heart pounding. The meanness of it stung.

Did someone in Riverbed resent her that much? Want her gone? No one in town had been anything but polite so far, but who knew who was holding a grudge against ... her? Her grandfather? Her grandmother for ditching the whole town?

Dust announced the arrival of Ray. He'd stayed at the Malory ranch last night, exhausted from rounding up the cattle. In fact, Drew hadn't expected him until this afternoon, but she was glad of his presence. He jogged over to her, surveying the damage.

Ray said nothing, but Drew saw the tightness in his eyes, the anger behind his silence.

He slid back his hat, wiping sweat from his forehead. "I'd blame the Haynes boys—they're vindictive like this—but Jarrod was taken into custody last night, and his brothers hightailed it. They must be nearly to Mexico by now."

"Why would anyone do this?" Drew hugged herself, hurting.

Ray put a comforting hand on her shoulder. "Don't know, sweetheart. Most folks are glad you're here. In fact, Craig Fuller is on his way with a load of supplies, and we're going to start on the basement. Electrician and plumber are on their way from White Fork, sent by Jack Hillman. They're grateful for the extra work."

As Ray finished, more dust rose into the sky in the wake of a delivery van and a work truck. Drew recognized Craig from the feed store as he hopped out of the van. The work truck held three guys, including Jack Hillman, clad in jeans and T-shirts, pulling on gloves as they ambled toward Ray, ready to start.

Each expressed dismay at the damage in their own way— one of the workers put his hands on his hips and spit into the grass, another shook his head. Craig said, "Aw, that *sucks.*"

Jack simply gazed at the house, as Ray had done. Then Jack began silently lifting the broken porch boards, sorting them into piles. Ray joined him.

By midmorning, the workers and Ray had torn out chunks of the basement, finding both a solid rock foundation and beams that had been put in not long ago. Someone had renovated at some time in the last twenty years, Ray told Drew when they took a break, removing asbestos and other hazards, leaving behind now-worn certificates that said it had been done.

Drew wondered about that. Had her grandfather tried to keep the place up and then found it beyond him? Or had he started renovating for a specific reason and then given up again?

Her fingertips tingled, the librarian in her wanting to know. An enjoyable part of her job had been doing historical research for patrons—libraries had resources that went well beyond the Internet.

Now she had her very own historical research project. Drew left the men to work and waded into the garage and the boxes of photos and documents she and Erica had barely made a dent in.

By the time Ray came in for lunch, she was sitting cross-legged on the new and beautiful garage floor, surrounded by piles of papers, newspapers, and photos.

"Hey, I just cleaned this place up," Ray joked as he crouched next to her. "What'cha doing?"

"Learning about my family." Drew indicated the file folder of newspaper clippings in her lap. "Grandma never talked about Riverbend, and my father didn't pay any attention to that part of his life."

"So, is the house haunted?" Ray sat down in the only clear space near her. "All the best old houses in Texas are haunted."

"If Grandfather's ghost is hanging around, he's being very quiet," Drew said. "I doubt *he* destroyed the porch."

"Naw, live humans did that. I found a crowbar, which I wrapped in a bag and sent to Ross's deputies to dust for fingerprints. Might not have anything he can use, but what the hell?"

Drew sent him a grateful look. "Thank you."

"My pleasure. Find anything interesting?"

"I think my grandmother might have wanted to marry someone else." Drew turned over a newspaper article showing a young woman with long hair arm-in-arm with a slim and handsome cowboy, who was definitely not Drew's grandfather. It was a gossipy article about how Abby Cole and a guy called Nick Travis were seen a lot together, she showing up at all his rodeo events. Wedding bells were sure to ring soon, the article said. The speculation had been repeated in other papers.

Ray peered at the blurry photo. "I don't recognize him. Not that I would from forty or so years ago, but I don't recognize the name either."

Drew ran her finger along the tiny type. "Says he's from Bastrop—that's over on the other side of Austin, isn't it? I wonder what happened. Did my grandmother dump him for Grandfather? Or did she like to flit from man to man? After all, she dumped Grandfather not long after she married him and my dad was born." Drew dropped the article back into the folder. "Or is there more to it than that?"

"There's always more to it. Life is complicated."

Ray touched her cheek, and Drew warmed with the contact. Her life was getting complicated, that was certain.

She put her hand on his. When he started to lift away, maybe thinking she pushed him off, she held on and tugged him closer.

Their mouths met in a hunger that hadn't abated. Whenever Erica stayed over with Faith, Ray and Drew snuggled together in bed, making love, whispering together, curling up and sleeping. It was a fine thing.

Finer was Ray's large hand pulling her close, his mouth opening hers, the quiet strength of his kiss. She could imbibe him forever and still not have enough.

"Whoa." A voice, young and male, floated energetically through the garage. "Sor-ree. I didn't mean to interrupt."

Ray took his time lifting away from Drew. No shame, no embarrassment.

A tall youth just out of his teens, towered inside the door. Drew had seen him around town—Manny Judd, employed by the horse rehab ranch Dr. Anna did vet work for.

Ray climbed leisurely to his feet and reached down to help Drew to hers. "Manny. What's up?"

"Ross sent me to look around and see if I can figure out who vandalized the house." A grin spread over his young face. "Send a criminal to catch a criminal, I guess. Hey, did they get in here too? It's a mess."

"No, that was me," Drew said. "Looking through old stuff."

Manny gave the papers an uninterested glance. "Where's the evidence?" he asked Ray.

"I'll show you." Ray winked at Drew. "Want to go into town with me and get some lunch?"

"Sure." Drew liked how easily he asked her, as though it was natural they'd grab lunch together.

She'd never had a relationship like this before. No awkward dates, no man trying to impress her with the restaurant he took her to, the important people he talked to on the phone while there, the way the restaurant employees treated him. Those dates had never been about Drew.

Ray simply wanted to have lunch with her. She hugged the fine feeling to herself as Ray took Manny off toward the house. Manny glanced back at Drew and gave her two thumbs-up.

TWO NIGHTS LATER, RAY PICKED UP DREW AND ERICA FOR A very special dinner at the diner.

Kyle had asked them to come. He'd plucked up his courage about Dr. Anna, Ray told her, and wanted the whole town there for his momentous evening.

No one had vandalized the house in the last couple

days, Ray's and the other men's work remaining untouched. Drew was amazed at how much they were getting done, but on the other hand, there was a long way to go.

Manny had hinted that he knew who had torn up the porch, but he'd touched his finger to his lips when asked and said he'd only discuss the case with Ross or his deputies until he knew for sure.

Manny was already at the diner when they arrived, inside with Deputy Harrison and his younger sister. Manny and Tracy Harrison were now a couple, Erica had informed Drew, proud she knew this intel.

As they approached the diner, the door swung open, and Kyle, in a fine suit, emerged with the agitated pace someone with a lot on his mind.

"What are you doing out here?" Ray asked him jovially when he reached them. "Food's in there."

Erica laughed in delight. "Good one, Ray."

Kyle, Drew could see, was too wound up for jokes. "Great to finally meet you, Drew," Kyle said, as Ray introduced them and he shook Drew's hand. "I've heard absolutely nothing about you."

Drew nodded, deadpan. "Ray can be a little quiet."

"I think Ray's pretty nice," Erica said. "You know, for an old guy."

Ray chuckled, and even Kyle brightened.

"Don't worry," Erica told Kyle as though imparting a great confidence. "Faith Sullivan says Dr. Anna's madly in love with you."

"*Erica.*" Drew flushed. "That's none of your business."

"Everyone knows," Erica said with her artlessness. "I love this town, even though I thought I'd hate it. There's a ton of stuff going on you'd never think in a nowhere place like this. Plus, it's really pretty."

"*Erica*," Drew repeated. "Sorry, Kyle. I did *not* teach her to be so rude."

Erica looked amazed. "Why is that rude? I said it was pretty."

"We're going inside." Drew put her hand on Erica's back. "Erica is quiet when she's eating."

Kyle managed a grin, but his face was wan, perspiration beading his forehead. Drew hoped he wouldn't bolt into the blue, but Ray put his hand on Kyle's shoulder, giving his brother a reassuring squeeze.

As Drew and Erica entered the diner, they were welcomed by Mrs. Ward, who led them to a seat. Ray hung back to speak briefly to Kyle, and Erica and Drew slid into the booth to wait for him.

"We need to have a talk, sweetie," Drew began to Erica. "There are things you say to people and things you don't."

Erica regarded her, wide-eyed across the table. "Even if it's the truth?"

"Sometimes especially if it's the truth. It's called discretion."

"Sounds boring."

At Erica's age, where the world was new, and endless possibilities stretched before her, keeping silent about … well, everything, probably was very difficult.

"She's okay," Ray said, joining them to hear the last part of the conversation. "Just friendly."

"Just consider what you say before you say it, Erica," Drew continued, having to keep being the mom. "Shouldn't be too hard."

Erica shrugged. "Okay."

Drew had no way of knowing if her words penetrated Erica's skull, but she let it go.

Ray lifted his hand to someone, and a pretty young woman came over. She wore a casual skirt and top but looked uncomfortable in them. Her dark hair was fetchingly unkempt, and her green eyes were the exact same shade as Ray's.

"Drew, this is Lucy. My baby sister. One of my baby sisters, I mean."

Drew slid out of the booth to greet her. "It's nice to meet you. Grace has told me a lot about you."

"Uh-oh," Lucy said with a hint of a smile, but her eyes held pain. "Grace has the dirt on everyone—in the nicest way. She's the good one. I'm the rebel."

Lucy didn't look rebellious at the moment, only sad.

"Want to join us?" Drew asked. "Or are you meeting someone?"

"Thanks, but Grace and Carter have already taken pity on me. Grace is trying to talk me into helping her out at her catering business, but what do I know about baking? I know horses and how to decorate an apartment on a shoestring."

Drew perked up. "Oh, do you think you could help *me* decorate the B&B? I have a tiny budget. Ray's great at helping out with the heavy work, but ..."

Lucy's amusement finally reached her eyes. "But he's a guy?" Her mirth faded. "It's sweet of you, Drew, but you don't have to keep me busy because of my sucky story."

"I don't know your story," Drew said. "Ray said you had a breakup and came home, no details, and Grace has kept your secrets to herself. I really do need the help. I can only do so many things at once."

Lucy hesitated, but seemed tempted. "Well ..."

"Please?" Erica said, giving her a hopeful look. "I want the B&B to be pretty so we can stay here."

Erica could do the poor-little-waif act very well. She gave Lucy puppy-dog eyes and let her lip tremble just enough.

Lucy relaxed. "Sure, I'll help you out. It might even be fun. Sorry," she said quickly. "I don't mean that like it sounds. I'm just in a bad place right now."

"I understand." Drew recalled the days after she'd finally parted from Philip. "It's like you're standing outside the world, looking in, as though none of the normal things are real anymore."

"Yeah." Lucy faltered, tears springing to her eyes. "That's it exactly."

Drew enfolded her in an impulsive hug. "But we get through it. That's what family is for."

She hadn't had much in the way of family to turn to herself, but she'd had Erica, and now she had the Malorys.

Lucy gave Drew a tight hug in return. "I'm going to leave now so I don't blubber. How about I come over to your place tomorrow, and we can talk decorating?"

Drew released her and nodded. "Looking forward to it."

She was, she realized. Drew liked Grace, but Lucy, instinct told her, would be the one she related to.

"She's pretty," Erica said as Lucy walked away. She had her eyes on Lucy's skirt and top and Drew had the feeling Erica would soon ask for an outfit just like it.

"That was nice of you," Ray said to Drew. "She really is upset. I'm about ready to bruise that ass—" He glanced at Erica, who listened avidly. "Butthole who hurt her like that."

"No, it was selfish of me," Drew said as she sat down again. "I really need the help."

"She'll be grateful. And it *was* nice." Ray reached over and covered Drew's hand with his.

The contact sent heat through her blood. Drew caught his gaze and saw the sinful promise in his eyes. Terrifying how easily she smiled at him, squeezed his hand in return, tried to send the promise back to him.

Ray was breaking down her barriers, making her question why she was so reticent and afraid of everything. His thumb moved on her hand, brushing the inside of her wrist, licking fire through her.

Barriers definitely falling.

"Ooh." Erica bounced in her seat. "There's Dr. Anna. She's here."

Chapter Fourteen

Ray was proud of his brother. He watched as Kyle bared his soul in front of the entire town, going down on one knee to propose to Anna.

And Anna said yes.

Ray put his arm around Drew as the diner cheered. He was glad for his brother—Kyle deserved happiness.

Kyle and Anna would move to the ranch, he figured. Anna's house was too small for them, especially if kids came along. She'd be closer to her vet clinic at the Malory place anyway.

That brought up the question—should Ray move out? Kyle and Anna would want their privacy. Lucy would land on her feet eventually and move on—she was unhappy now, but the Malory sisters were no wilting weeds. Lucy would figure out what she wanted to do and head back into the world again.

Ray glanced at Drew, who laughed and applauded Anna and Kyle with the rest of the town. Erica did a wild dance in the aisle with Faith and Dominic, her long limbs flying.

Ray wasn't one for analyzing relationships, but he wondered what was between himself and Drew. Two lonely people having a thing? Or was there something more to it?

He could easily fall in love with her. He mused on Drew's pretty eyes, her laugh, the way she adored her daughter. Her resilience, her need to do things for the right reason. The way she looked at Ray as though she saw him as a person in his own right, not a cowboy or a rodeo star, a man good for a quick roll in the hay before she sought the next guy.

Ray's body heated as her eyes went starry, her happiness for Kyle and Anna apparent.

Yep, in love. Hard, fast, and absolute.

———

LUCY LEFT THE DINER EARLY AND ALONE. SHE WAS HAPPY FOR Kyle and loved Dr. Anna, but she wanted some space to process things.

She'd been so damned proud of herself for her brilliant job in Houston. She'd handled investments for large corporations, responsible for billions of dollars, and she'd done it well.

So proud Clyde had chosen *her* to be on his arm at fundraising dinners and opera openings, even though society pages the next day listed them as "Mr. Clyde Gordon and companion." As though she was from an escort service or something.

Didn't matter, she'd reasoned. One day the papers would list them as Mr. Clyde Gordon and Mrs. Lucy Malory-Gordon.

Sure.

For a long time, Lucy had been the one with the

successful relationship, and she'd been a little smug about it. Now Grace, Kyle, and Ray had become parts of a couple— Ray and Drew were together even if Ray hadn't admitted it yet.

Lucy was the one alone.

She kept telling herself how happy she was for Kyle, and Grace and Carter with their new baby, and Ray with Drew, and she truly was, deep down. But she also felt sorry for herself.

The bar was a good place to go after the diner. Nice to be in a town where it wasn't weird to go to the bar by yourself. When Lucy walked in, half the place greeted her, and she knew she'd soon find old friends to talk to and share a few beers with.

The big cowboy, Hal Jenkins, turned from the bar as she entered and gave her a nod. "Lucy."

"Hey." Lucy took the barstool next to him and ordered a beer. Hal was comforting to be around—he didn't demand scintillating conversation or care she wasn't dressed to the nines with her hair perfect. "How's it going?"

"It's going." Hal had once been a bull rider, and good at it, winning plenty of trophies and prize money. He now was a ranch manager, doing that just as well.

Lucy took her beer from the bartender but lingered, the two drinking in silence a moment.

"Cool about Kyle and Anna," Hal said.

He wasn't just making conversation, Lucy knew. Hal didn't speak unless he had something he thought worth saying.

"Yes." Lucy sounded too bright. "Anna is wonderful. I heard she even got into the ring as a rodeo clown."

"Yep. She wanted to see the bull riding from the ground,

so to speak, so she asked me to help her out." Hal gave her a slow grin. "She wasn't bad at it. But then, Anna's great with animals." He paused. "I'm including Kyle in that statement."

They both laughed, Lucy feeling her tightness loosen a little. But she didn't want it to, fearing she'd cry, so she shut it off and took a gulp of beer.

Hal leaned closer. His voice dropped, wrapping them in a bubble of privacy.

"I know what you went through—Ray told me a little. Not that I'll talk about it far and wide. I just want you to know that if you need anything, you ask me."

"Oh." Lucy blinked at him.

She'd known Hal all her life, but she hadn't paid much attention to him. He'd simply been one of her brother's friends. Now she noted his brown eyes, intense and dark under close-buzzed black hair, the short beard he'd grown since she'd seen him last, his powerful shoulders and work-worn hands.

"Thanks," she said awkwardly. "That's sweet."

Hal's brows came together. "It's not *sweet*. I mean it." He withdrew, moving back to his bottle of beer. "I'll be around. Your brothers know how to get hold of me."

"Okay." The word was faint.

Did he mean he'd help out as a friend—as Drew had offered, as Anna had? Or was he hinting at something more? Hal was like Ray—cryptic as hell.

Lucy had been burned and burned badly, but as she sat on the barstool, soothed by Hal's silence, she wondered if, once she healed, the man on her right would be a balm for her hurts.

Drew entered the town library on Monday, notebook and pencil in hand. Erica loved her phone and tablet, but Drew liked making notes with pencil and paper. She found that the act of writing by hand helped her remember things better.

The library was larger than she'd thought it would be, much bigger than the branch that had employed her. The two-story building had been built for the express purpose of being a library, so said the plaque outside the fan-lighted front door. The interior boasted a wide staircase with a polished banister and row after row of books.

A *real* library, Drew thought with a thrill as she entered. One that smelled like old paper, dust motes, and time.

The librarian was a solid-looking woman with red and blue streaks in her gray hair. Her assistants were younger, one of whom gave Drew an eager smile, ready to help.

When Drew asked the assistant her question, the librarian, Dena, pushed over. "Town history is in that section." She pointed to a shadowy corner under the staircase. "What are you looking for, specifically?"

"Anything about my grandparents," Drew said. "I have photos and newspaper clippings they left behind, but I'm not sure how to put it all together. If I could see the original newspapers or digital copies …"

"Digital?" Dena chortled. "I've been bugging the county for funding to digitize our archives for years. They might get to it by the next century. Microfilm and microfiche is what we have here, as well as old hard copies, what is still intact. I don't suppose you know how to work a microfiche machine?"

"Of course. I'm a librarian myself."

"Ah." Dena peered at her more closely, the bond of

kinship that united librarians of the world linking Drew in. "Then you'll understand my frustration."

"I do. What we need, and what they want to fund is never the same."

"Welcome to Riverbend, honey. Of course, in this town, if you want to know about the past, you ask people. They never forget."

Drew thought about Mrs. Kaye, who'd seemed to know all about her grandparents. Dena had a point.

"I've found plenty of photos and articles about my grandfather and the B&B," Drew said, "but only a little about my grandmother. I knew *her*—she passed away when I was a kid—but I don't know much about her past. She never talked about her life before she moved to Chicago. My father never talked about it either, if he even knew, and I was too young to notice or be interested. Maybe if I could speak to any friends she had..."

"She didn't have many," Dena said, her tone turning dark. "Don't be upset if you encounter some resistance from people to open up about her. As I say, Riverbend has a long memory."

Drew regarded her in surprise. "Because she left my grandfather?"

"She did so much more, honey, I'm sorry to say." Dena put her hand on Drew's arm and steered her toward a polished door in the back of the library. "Let's go somewhere we can talk."

RAY WATCHED DREW DRIVE OFF ON HER QUEST AT THE LIBRARY after Carter Sullivan had swung by to pick Erica up for school. Carter was the designated driver who toted Faith, Dominic, and now Erica to the elementary school.

Ray nodded to him, and Carter nodded back, the two men not needing to exchange words.

Erica, on the other hand, was already chattering as she jumped into the truck with her new friends. "Hey, Carter, guess what we found in the basement yesterday …"

Ray and Jack had uncovered beautiful solid oak paneling that could be pried out and saved to either panel the rest of the house, or—Ray's idea—be made into doors and furniture for the new B&B. Drew had been happy they'd found something positive. Things were moving forward, one baby step at a time.

Ray, Jack, and Jack's guys got to work to finish clearing out the basement. The electrician had come on Friday, looked around, and announced the whole house had to be redone—no surprise. Now Jack's workers were charting out what would go where. Ray found the generator, with no fuel, of course, and drove into town to get some.

He spotted Drew in the town square. She stood on the green in front of the courthouse, staring at the building, while townsfolk strolled past her, sending her curious glances.

Ray slowed his truck. "Hey," he called out the open window. "Couldn't find the library?"

He liked how Drew's face lit up when she saw him, how she smiled as she approached his truck. "Oh, I found it." Her brief delight faded. "I think I found out too much."

Ray did not like her unhappy look. "Want to grab some lunch?"

Drew grimaced. "I don't know if I want to sit in the diner

right now. I'd have to be friendly to everyone. One thing I miss about the city is I can be anonymous if I want."

That bad, was it? Ray considered. "Tell you what. How about we pick something up at Grace's bakery and have a little picnic. Just you and me."

The smile returned. "I'd like that." Drew put her hand on his truck's door handle then hesitated. "I left my car at the library."

Which was a block away. "No one will touch it. Hop in."

Drew climbed readily into the big truck, and Ray drove round the corner. He parked a few spaces down from the bakery, and Drew burst out laughing.

"I could have walked here. It's what, a hundred feet from where we just were?"

"But I'm a gentleman," Ray said as he hopped out to go around and open her door. "I couldn't tell you to walk and meet me here."

Drew slid out, almost into his arms. "Yes, you could have."

"Not my way." Ray slammed the door and guided her to the bakery.

"I know. You're a gentleman." Drew looked pleased rather than exasperated, which pleased *him*.

They ordered from Grace's young assistant, who cheerfully handed them a bag of croissant sandwiches, teacakes, and profiteroles. Ray drove with Drew out of town and down a side road near the Malory ranch, to a meadow edged with trees.

"It's beautiful," Drew breathed as she climbed from the truck.

"Yep." Ray opened the pickup's tailgate. "We'll have the picnic in here. Grass will be muddy and full of chiggers." He made a mental note to stash some blankets in his truck for next time.

Drew unwrapped her sandwich from its paper and took a bite. "Mmm," she said in true enjoyment. "This is *good.*" She eyed Ray's elegant croissant sandwich, almost lost in his big hand, and laughed. "Not really cowboy food."

Ray shrugged. "I've been eating this stuff most of my life. Grace makes a mean steak, but she's also good at the dainty, girly food." He grinned around a bite of sandwich. "Me and Kyle love it," he said. "Don't tell on us."

Drew laughed again, whatever had made her unhappy lifted for the moment. They shared the tiny cakes and the profiteroles, cream dabbing Drew's lips.

Ray leaned over and licked it off.

Drew softened under him, her mouth meeting his in a kiss. The kiss went on, Ray sliding an arm around her and drawing her close.

She tasted like sunshine and sweet cream. Ray's mind conjured images of him smearing the cream across her skin and feasting on her. Then he'd encourage her to do the same to him.

Her mouth was hot, body pliant against his. Ray rested his hand on her thigh, remembering how she'd snuggled against him the last time they'd shared her bed, her legs draping his.

He wished he could do that always.

The breeze sharpened, reminding Ray that they sat outdoors for the world to see.

He put a finger under her chin. "Time to tell me what's upset you."

Drew let out a long sigh. "The past. Lies."

"Lies about what?"

"My family." Drew set down her profiterole and leaned against him. "Ones *they* told, I mean. I went to the library today and met Dena. She took me into her office to talk, and she called Mrs. Ward—I didn't realize the two were sisters. Mrs. Ward came over, and they told me about my grandmother."

Ray had a feeling they hadn't told her anything good. He didn't know much about the Pareskys, but Mrs. Ward and Dena, who interacted with everyone in town, would have the dirt.

"Mrs. Ward and her sister are a generation younger than my grandparents, but they remember," Drew went on. "*Their* parents talked a lot about them, and Dena said she listened hard. Apparently my grandmother was a wild child. This was in a decade women in small towns didn't do *anything* but settle down and get married. She was a rebel." Drew smiled, a bit proudly. "I remember that Grandmother was never conventional. Didn't let her hair go gray or stay home to bake cookies. She ran in marathons until she made the choice not to, went to blues concerts, worked at the Art Institute, sponsored artists, had a ton of friends. Grandmother loved the city and city life. I can see why she didn't fit in around here."

"There wasn't much choice for girls in Riverbend back in the day," Ray agreed. "People were hard on ones who didn't toe the line. Hell, they still can be."

"Dena and Mrs. Ward looked at me hard today. I could almost hear them wondering if I'll turn out to be more like my grandfather or my grandmother."

"Neither one," Ray said. "You're just you."

"I'm realizing why I like you." Drew snuggled into him, putting her arm through his. "Anyway, Mrs. Ward told me about the 'Big Scandal'." She made air quotes with one hand. "My grandfather had always been in love with my grandmother. He chased her, and she spurned him. Then one day, she suddenly accepted his proposal, and they married a week later. End of story, right? But she had a baby eight months later, and people can count. Yes, babies can come prematurely, but my dad was full-term and healthy. Nurses at the clinic confirmed that. Half the town decided she and my grandfather'd had a little fun before the wedding, but the other half knew Grandmother had been seeing a cowboy on the rodeo circuit—the one called Nick Travis I showed you the article about. She'd even followed the rodeo earlier that season, and who knew what she got up to, and with whom? So Dena said."

"They think she was a buckle bunny?" Ray asked in surprise.

"Apparently. It's hard to imagine, because I only knew her when she was in her sixties. But no one's born old, are they? She was restless and wanted adventure, probably. Erica is a lot like her." Drew made a face. "Uh-oh. I should keep an eye on her."

"Erica's a good kid, and this is the twenty-first century. Little different. Though we still have buckle bunnies," he conceded.

"So you can guess what people believed," Drew went on. "She was seen with this cowboy, all over him, from eyewitness accounts, and then he disappears. Next thing you know, my grandfather is marrying her."

"And she's having a baby." Ray nodded. "And people wonder whether the kid was your grandad's or the cowboy's."

"Exactly."

"Huh." Ray went silent, thinking it through. "Could be why she and your grandfather split up."

"That's what Dena said. Maybe he figured it out, she said, and was naturally upset that the boy he thought his son wasn't his. Whatever happened, Grandmother took my dad and left town, the state—the whole southern half of the U.S. She never, ever talked about my grandfather or Riverbend. I spent the first part of my life thinking my grandfather was dead. No one ever told me that. I just assumed."

Ray pushed back his hat, letting his forehead cool. "Are they sure? I saw those pictures of your grandparents you showed me, and you look kind of like your grandfather. Same eyes."

"You think so? I always looked like my dad more than my mom—but how can we know when we only have old fuzzy photos to go by?"

Ray had taken plenty of time to memorize Drew's eyes, and would know similar ones when he saw them.

"If your dad *wasn't* Paresky's kid," Ray said slowly. "What does this mean about property your granddad left you? Is that even a question?"

"I don't think so, but I'm not sure. My grandfather's name is on my dad's birth certificate—Dena said the nurses at the clinic confirmed that. So, legally, my grandfather is listed as my dad's father, which means he didn't openly dispute the patrimony. Maybe he didn't want to, for fear of the truth, or maybe he didn't want my father to be hurt."

"Your grandfather left you the B&B," Ray said. "Which means he thought of you as his granddaughter, and his heir. The trust named you specifically, right?"

"Yes. Not just his grandchild, but me by name. But the fact that my dad might not have been my grandfather's could

explain why Grandfather set such harsh terms. I save the
B&B and make it run, or I lose it. If I'm not his blood relation, I need to work for it."

"Maybe." Ray had a different idea, but he said nothing. He
had no proof, only an old photo and the joy of looking into
Drew's eyes.

"A bit depressing finding all this out," Drew said. "I wish
my grandmother could have *told* me all this, or at least told
my dad. I don't think he knew. He was only about two years
old when he and my grandmother left Riverbend."

"She didn't want to hurt him," Ray suggested. "Or she
wanted to forget about it and live her life."

Drew kissed Ray's chin. "I'm sorry. I imagine this makes
you think of you and Christina."

"Sort of," Ray said, uncomfortable. "Not really the same
thing, though."

"At least she told you."

"Yeah, she did," Ray said. "I've always admired her for
being honest. But trust me when I say I'm real glad Christina
is with Grant."

"They seem happy. And Emma is sure cute."

"Yeah, that." Ray brushed Drew's face, turning her to look
at him. "And it left me free when I met you."

A flush stole across Drew's cheeks, one Ray hoped meant
pleasure. He leaned to her and kissed her slowly, putting an
end to the conversation in the best way he knew how.

WHEN THEY RETURNED TO THE B&B, DREW IN HER OWN CAR,
Manny came racing from the house and the men working
there to meet them.

"Ray. Drew. Sure am glad to see you. You took forever getting home."

Drew opened her mouth to ask him what was wrong, but Manny plunged on, excited and impatient.

"I think I figured out who wrecked your place the other night. But I can't prove it. I wanna set a trap for them and have Ross catch their asses. That okay with you?"

Chapter Fifteen

⁂

Manny's idea for a trap consisted of Drew and Ray conspicuously going out and leaving the house unguarded. Meanwhile, Manny would lie in wait and pounce on the vandals when they arrived.

Drew supposed Manny thought he'd knock out the guys and tie them up, single-handedly, to present to the sheriff. Or maybe to Deputy Harrison, to impress the brother of his girlfriend.

"Not by yourself," Drew told him. "Too dangerous." When Manny started to look hurt, she quickly added. "You need someone to have your back."

Ray gave Manny a nod. "Jack will do it. He's not happy about the vandalism."

Manny brightened. "Yeah, Jack's a badass. We'll take 'em down."

Ray nodded as if all was settled. Erica would spend the night with Faith—she was becoming a regular at Circle C Ranch—and Drew and Ray would go out and stay late.

When Riverbenders wanted to make a night of it, Drew

was coming to understand, they went to the diner and then the bar, or else the touristy cowboy bar, Dino's. Special occasions warranted a drive to White Fork and the restaurant Chez Orleans, or a longer drive into Austin or San Antonio.

Ray suggested the diner and bar, because they'd be close if something happened. Drew agreed. This wasn't a date, she reminded herself, but the pretense of a date. No dressing up and sitting at a table loaded with silverware—Philip used to deride her if she picked up the wrong fork.

"The diner sounds great," Drew said. "I need more of that harvest apple pie before the season ends."

They finished up work for the day. Drew changed into a cute skirt she'd been saving, and Ray, after giving her a smile that promised much for later, led her out to the truck.

"You kids have fun," Manny said as he waved them off. Jack stood near the house, looking around far more seriously, which relieved Drew. She didn't know Jack well yet, but she believed he'd keep an eye on Manny.

"Don't be *too* good," Manny yelled, and Ray chuckled as he started the truck.

"I think I used to be that full of shit," he said, pulling out. "Seems like a long time ago now."

He didn't sound sad—he was just stating a fact.

For now, Drew had a full evening with him. Though Ray had been staying at the house most of the time, she hadn't seen much of him. He worked all day and far into the night, often showering and dropping off to sleep on the couch, a nice one he'd brought from his own house, after she'd gone to bed.

Like a real married couple, she'd think wryly.

No, that was too flip. Ray was working his ass off helping

out without asking for payment. She was grateful and shouldn't expect more.

But then she'd think of how they'd lain together in her bed more than once, wrapped in sunshine and each other and content. How they'd kissed lazily in the meadow during their impromptu picnic. She loved how she and Ray came together so easily, untroubled. No discussing it, no taking stock of what they'd done and where this relationship was going. No analyzing it to death. Simply enjoying each other in the autumn days, no worries of what winter might bring.

At the diner Ray's conversation turned to the house and what he and his team were finding—wiring was shot, yeah, but they'd discovered decent plumbing pipes, great old wood, beams that were solid, with only a few that needed replacing, like the ones that had crashed down on them in the dining room.

"Sorry, I'm rambling," Ray said after a time. "What'd you usually talk about with your boyfriends in Chicago? The latest musicals? Or am I confusing it with New York?"

Drew moved her fork through the whipped cream on the largest slice of apple pie she'd had here yet. "The same stuff everyone talks about in Riverbend. What our kids are doing, fixing up our houses or apartments. TV shows, movies, and sports. People are mostly the same everywhere—I'm getting that now."

Ray's eyes glinted with humor. "What'd you expect? That cowboys would chew on strands of hay and spit through our teeth?"

"Pretty much. That's the picture painted of life in a ranch town."

"And we say *shucks, ma'am.* If we aren't saying *ain't* and *Well, dayum.*"

"Manny says *Well, dayum,*" Drew pointed out. "I've heard him. And *ain't.*"

"He picks it up from television."

They laughed together. So nice, Drew thought. Sharing laughter, anecdotes about friends. Someone to be with, to go through life with. That was true love.

She stilled, the thought jolting through her.

Love. Not wild passion that dropped her on her ass and left her bereft. She'd been madly in love with Philip, which had blinded her to the kind of person he'd truly been. Witty and smart, she'd thought, when he'd just been plain mean and trivializing.

Not that passion with Ray hadn't been wild. It was over-the-top wild, and Drew wanted to experience it again, many times over. Whenever Ray smiled at her, eyes warm, her body heated in anticipation.

Ray grounded her at the same time, protecting her while she rode the fire with him. They'd reach their peaks together, and she'd not felt alone for an instant when making love with Ray.

To distract herself from grabbing Ray and jumping his bones right there, she glanced around the diner, pleased she already recognized so many faces. Clint, who did the announcing at the local rodeos. Mrs. Kaye, the older woman who'd known her grandparents. Polly, who helped out at Grace's bakery. Hal Jenkins, the ranch hand, eating by himself. Drew had seen the way he'd looked at Lucy … might be something in that.

Her gaze rested on a booth holding five people she hadn't

seen before. "Strangers in town," she said in a low voice, motioning with her fork. "Could they be our vandals?"

The strangers in question were three men and two women who didn't speak much as they shoveled in chicken-fried steak and mashed potatoes. They wore beat up jeans and shirts, or cargo shorts with bulging pockets.

Ray twisted around to look, not hiding his stare. "Oh, those are the archaeologists," he said, righting himself and lifting his coffee. "Some of them, anyway. They come into town from time to time."

"Archaeologists?" Drew raised her brows. "What are they excavating?"

"Ancient Native Americans," Ray answered. "I asked them about it once. They've found traces of settlements from ten thousand years ago or so in the caves up around the river. Makes sense. River Country is a nice place to live. Probably was back then too."

"The archaic period." Drew's inner librarian awoke. "We have mounds in Illinois with all kinds of artifacts—I went with Erica a couple times on field trips. North America has civilizations going back thousands and thousands of years, had cities as organized and sophisticated as any in Ancient Rome." She broke off as she found Ray's eyes on her. "Sorry. I'm a history nerd. Occupational hazard."

"It's cool you know all that stuff. Erica's going to grow up smart."

"She's already very smart. The problem is, she knows it." Drew softened in fondness. "I'm blessed with a wonderful kid. As pissed off as I ever got at Philip, I was grateful for Erica."

"You should be." Ray took a sip of coffee, unworried.

"Does it bug you when I talk about Philip?" Drew asked, watching him.

Ray carefully set down his cup. "What bugs me is he was such a bastard to you. I can't believe he didn't understand or appreciate what he had. I'm glad you broke up with him. I'm sorry he died, mostly because it makes you feel guilty."

"I don't know why it does." Drew turned her cup on the table, the pie long gone. "It wasn't my fault he'd decided to drive to Milwaukee. I didn't even know."

"And one day, you'll be able to let that go. When my dad died of a heart defect, I blamed myself out the butt, though wasn't a thing I could have done. He was born with the problem, and lived as much as he could while he could. Took me a long time to understand all that, but eventually I did." He touched her hand. "It's not a door you can just close. I kept trying that, and beating myself up when it didn't work. Time's the only cure. And living your life."

"Yeah." Drew caressed his fingers. "Living."

They shared a long look, then Ray said, "Tell you what. Let's get out of here and go do some dancing. Less depressing."

"You dance?" Drew looked him up and down.

"I've been known to."

They left the booth and Ray held her hand as he walked with her to the register. He paid for Drew's meal, in front of God and everybody, and Mrs. Ward gave them an indulgent smile.

Halfway to the bar, Drew stopped. "I just remembered. I *don't* dance. I don't know how."

"That's okay." Ray drew her close and led her on, music blaring from inside the bar. "I'll teach you."

DREW HAD SEEMED SURPRISED RAY KNEW HOW TO DANCE, BUT he'd been two-stepping around floors since junior high. Around here, a guy who could dance had plenty of girl-friends.

He had Drew laughing as he showed her how to catch the rhythm. It was a good dance, the two-step, where a couple could be close but still get into the beat.

She didn't mind at all that he kept hold of her hand as the dance ended and they moved to a table, sipping drinks the bartender brought. Wouldn't be much drinking, because they needed to stay alert—more dancing would help with that.

Ray wished this date was real and not about catching vandals at the B&B. He wanted to have Drew here with him as his girl, the one who smiled at him as they spun slowly around the dance floor.

By midnight, when they hadn't heard a word from the B&B, Ray suggested they go home. He realized as he said it that it didn't matter whether they went to the Malory ranch or the B&B or a tent in the middle of nowhere—home would be where Drew was.

The B&B was quiet when they reached it. Ray parked, and as he and Drew entered the garage, Jack appeared from the shadows.

"Nothing yet," Jack said, his voice a low rumble. "Manny swears they have something planned for tonight. He's posi-tive, he keeps saying. Tell you what—turn off all the lights when you go upstairs and make like you're not paying atten-tion to the rest of the world." His teeth flashed in a grin, the silver earring on his lobe sparkling.

"Good advice," Drew said lightly, moving past him and up the stairs.

Jack started to laugh, but suppressed it. "Lucky bastard," he whispered to Ray.

Ray growled at him and went up the stairs after Drew.

As Ray suspected, Drew was far too shy to make love when she knew Jack and Manny waited below. But she didn't mind snuggling up to Ray in bed, watching moonlight and shadows shimmer on the ceiling.

Ray drifted to sleep, hard and unfulfilled in body, but the rest of him pretty happy. He had Drew's hair across his shoulder, her even breath brushing his skin, her body curled into his. He'd found a place of his own right here with her.

Around dawn, shouts sounded outside, and Ray jumped awake, Drew sitting up in sleepy alarm. Ray heard Jack's gruff voice and Manny laughing. Flashing red and blue lights leaked through the shutters to stain the morning.

Ray and Drew scrambled out of bed and into their clothes, and Ray led the way downstairs.

Ross and Deputies Harrison and Sanchez surrounded three teen boys Ray recognized from White Fork. They were big guys, sandy-haired—cousins—and looked furious.

They didn't protest their innocence. Sanchez and Harrison were removing tools of destruction from their hands—crowbars, sledgehammers, bricks. The caved in door on the B&B was more evidence they'd been caught in the act.

"You're dead, Judd," one of the boys snarled at Manny.

Manny didn't look worried. "Your folks can afford good lawyers—you'll be fine. Just cough up who put you up to this and I bet Sheriff Campbell will go easy on you."

Ross looked irritated, but he only gave the teens his

steady stare, the one that made hardened criminals back down. Baby Campbell was no soft touch.

Ray didn't know if it was Ross's grim look or the sight of Ray and Jack looming out of the darkness that made the boys break. The younger one took a step behind the others.

"It was some dude," the oldest boy said. "I don't know him —he's not from River County. But he said he'd pay us five thousand dollars. *Five thousand.* Enough to get us out of this dump."

"Name?" Ross asked. "Don't worry. You'll be safe from him in jail."

The older boy shivered. "I don't give a rat's ass about him. Like I said, he wasn't from around here. I don't know his last name. He told us to call him Bolo. Stupid."

Ray heard Drew's gasp. He turned quickly and found her face ashen in the flickering lights.

"What is it, baby? You okay?"

"Jules," she whispered. "Bolo was his nickname. His and Philip's both."

"Shit," Ray said softly. What the hell was Drew's brother-in-law doing wrecking her house? What was it to him that Drew didn't succeed?

Right now wasn't the time for those questions. Drew was hurting. He put his arms around her and pulled her in.

Chapter Sixteen

Jack Hillman rode to town after Ross wrapped things up at the B&B. He was cramped and tired after his night of the stakeout, which made him cranky. He was glad it had been resolved—those idiot boys needed to learn they couldn't get away with anything they wanted—but he had to open his own business at ten, and there wasn't much chance of shuteye between now and then.

It didn't improve his temper to pull up on the corner of a row of pretty painted houses in White Fork to see Deke stomp out of one of them and explode at Karen.

Jack turned his motorcycle down her street to let it idle in front of her house. He wore the half helmet he liked—gave him protection but let him look around without restriction. He scowled at Deke as the young cowboy lit up the neighborhood with his half-drunk, half-hungover foul language.

Karen, fully dressed in a business suit despite the early hour, listened patiently from her porch.

"The truck is yours, honey," she said. "Take it and go. Stop waking up my neighbors."

"That's *your* fault." Deke thrust a thick finger in her direction. "You are making a big mistake, sweetheart. It's not every guy like me who'd take up with an old bitch like—*oof.*"

Deke's words choked off as Jack, who'd quietly slipped from his bike, got one arm around Deke's thick neck. Deke was plenty strong, but he was unsteady from a night full of beer, and Jack knew exactly how to bring down even a big guy like Deke.

"She told you to go," Jack said in a quiet voice, staring into Deke's confused eyes. "Get the hell out of this town and don't let me see you in it again."

Deke puffed up belligerently, but then he saw something in Jack's gaze that made him ease back.

"Fine, fine. I'm going. No reason for me to stay. Are you fucking her now? Is that what's going on?"

Jack turned Deke around and shoved him off the porch. Deke flailed as he landed on the sidewalk, regained his footing, and marched to his gleaming pickup with what dignity he could.

Deke looked back as he reached the truck. He opened his mouth as though to make a parting shot, caught Jack's deadly gaze, and quickly closed it again. The pickup roared to life once Deke hopped into the driver's seat, and Deke squealed away. He rounded the corner at high speed, nearly tipping the truck, but he righted it and zoomed off with a street-shaking rumble.

Jack watched him go. "I notice he wasn't too proud to walk away from the truck."

Karen studied the corner around which Deke had disappeared. "Can't blame him. It's a nice truck." She switched her focus to Jack. "You look awful. Want some coffee?"

Jack unstrapped his helmet and pulled it and his

sunglasses off. "Coffee sounds great."

He followed Karen into a pristine designer world. Her house had polished hardwood floors, a boxy sofa and chairs in a tweedy gray material, stainless steel appliances, and a refrigerator made to look like the rest of the cabinets.

Sunlight poured through the windows, plantation shutters open, and gleamed on the surfaces. The only softness in the place was an orange striped cat who'd stretched itself out across the back of the sofa.

The cat was such a weird note in the chill surroundings, that Jack peered closely at it to see if it was real. The cat opened one brilliant green eye, gave him a vaguely interested stare, and closed the eye again.

Karen lifted two mugs from a glass-fronted cabinet and set them on the immaculate counter, filling them with fragrant coffee from her latest model coffee machine.

"You going to tell me why you're riding around at five in the morning looking like hell?" Karen asked as she handed him the mug. Her hair was neatly arranged, like her suit. Jack couldn't help imagining her with hair coming out of the French braid, her jacket off, blouse unbuttoned. No wonder Deke didn't want to go.

"Catching vandals." Jack explained briefly, and Karen nodded with satisfaction and sympathy.

"Poor Drew. I'll have to make sure she's okay."

"Ray's with her." Jack lifted his mug. "That's going somewhere, I think. What about you? Why the hell do you go out with guys like Deke?"

Something flashed in Karen's brown eyes, which she suppressed with a shrug and smile. "Why else? He's cute and sexy."

"What you mean is, you can have control over him and

end it when you want. No matter what *he* thinks."

Again the flash of … Anger? Irritation? Sorrow? "It's easier that way."

"For you, sure." Jack took a sip of coffee. "Out of curiosity, why don't you try going out with a real guy? You know, not a rodeo star barely out of his mama's house?"

"You mean a man who wants me to fawn over him and his corner office when I know I'm smarter than he is and better at making money? Pretend I'm a quiet little nobody so I won't step on his ego? Be there for him when *he* wants me and be invisible when he doesn't?"

"No." Jack set down his coffee and took a step closer to her. "I mean a *real* guy. One you can talk to. One who gets you."

"I've never met anyone like that." Karen's eyes narrowed. "Or do you mean a *real guy* as in you?"

Jack shrugged, his chest tightening. "Why not me? I'm not a stud who thinks his dick is bigger than the truck you give him, and I don't give a shit if you make more money than I do. I have a business, and I'm happy with it. I don't have to take beautiful women out to dinner to prove to myself I'm not a loser."

"So you'd rather take an old bitch like me?" Karen gave him a wintery smile. "Like Deke tried to say?"

"Deke can suck it." Jack took another step, close enough to reach out and touch her if he decided to. "You're not an old bitch. Not old anyway—you *can* be bitchy, and you know it and like it. Take a chance, Karen. Go out with someone you can actually talk to."

"What am I going to talk about with you? Motorcycles?"

"Whatever the hell you want."

Karen's lips parted, as though she'd give him another

smart-ass retort, but her expression turned wistful. "I used to ride," she surprised him by saying. "A long time ago. I gave up bikes because I had to keep my dresses nice for meetings and looking good on the arm of my stupid husband of the moment."

"There you go."

Her eyes sharpened again. "And then what? You brag around town that you banged Karen Marvin? Who only dates hot cowboys younger than twenty-eight?"

"You're seriously all about yourself, aren't you?"

As Karen glared at him, Jack saw the sorrow he'd sensed before, and also trepidation. This was a woman who'd been burned and burned bad. She dated guys like Deke and tossed them aside when she got bored, so she wouldn't be hurt. If she never involved herself with someone she might truly like, she'd be safe.

And lonely as hell. No one ever said the words "lonely" and "Karen Marvin" in the same sentence, but Jack, who said little and saw much, knew she was.

"Tell you what," he said, gentling his tone. "Go out with me. We'll ride, we'll eat, whatever. No banging. Not even any fondling. We can hang out, see if we like it."

His body kicked him as soon as the words came out. What was he saying? Take out a gorgeous woman like Karen and not touch her? He had to be seriously tired.

Karen regarded him with new respect and a little bit of hope. She flicked her fingers as though nonchalant. "Sure. But if I'm to be hanging on the back of your bike, what am I supposed to wear? Black leather catsuit?"

Jack's zipper got tight as the flash came to him of Karen in skintight black leather, her golden hair windswept, her eyes glinting in good humor.

He swallowed and shook his head. "No fake biker-chick shit. Just wear something comfortable. If you used to ride, you'll know."

Karen's teasing faded. "I remember. Now finish your coffee. I have to go. Business to run."

"Yeah, me too." Jack drained his mug of the seriously good coffee, set it in the sink, and ran water into it.

When Karen looked astonished that he'd actually rinse out his own cup, he grinned at her, threaded one hand through her hair as she leaned next to him, and kissed her on the mouth.

Brief, warm, soft, sleek, a touch of lips and not much more. But enough that Jack tasted coffee, and nervousness, and anticipation.

"See you, Karen," he made himself say, and took himself out of the house.

He expected her to call something after him, some cutting remark about him messing up her hair, or thinking he was irresistible, but she said nothing.

Jack fought the temptation to look back at the house and her on the porch as he settled his helmet and started up his bike. He rode away, his heart thumping hard, and noticed his hands were shaking.

DREW CALLED JULES'S CELL NUMBER AND GOT NO ANSWER. He'd know it was her, so she left a message, deciding to pretend she didn't realize he'd tried to sabotage her house.

"How are you, Jules? Can you give me a call?" She hung up, quivering in anger. "You total betraying, gutless bastard."

Ray set a steaming cup of coffee in front of her, understanding and just as angry. "The kids told Ross your brother-in-law called or texted them with instructions—they never saw him face to face. Which means he might be hiding out nearby … or still in Chicago."

"He'd have to pay them. How did he plan to do that?"

Ray's grim mouth softened. "PayPal. Which means it might be very easy to prove his connection with them. Unless he's smart enough to set up a bogus account and bogus credit card."

Drew sat up straighter. "I bet he simply planned not to pay them at all. Jules is good at making promises he doesn't keep. They'd never met him, don't know where he's from, and he only gave them his nickname—what could they do?"

"You said it was your husband's nickname too," Ray said, curious. "How'd that work?"

Drew rolled her eyes, remembering. "A play on their last name of Bolan. Bolo One and Bolo Two. Philip was One. When I first met Philip, I thought it was cute." She wrinkled her nose. "It got annoying seriously quick."

Ray's grin lit his face. "They called themselves Number One and Number Two? Man, you could have had fun with that."

Drew started to feel better. "I did once. They were furious." Philip had been icy to her for a week. "Worth it."

"Stop me if I ever want to take a stupid nickname. Ray is bad enough."

"I like Ray." Drew slid her fingers over his. "Like Little Ray of Sunshine."

Ray choked and set down his cup. He grabbed her hand. "Oh, hell, no."

"How about Hot Cowboy?" Drew rose to meet him. "I like that one."

Ray pulled her closer. "Just don't say it in front of Kyle. Or my sisters. Or my friends. Well, anyone."

Drew went up on her tiptoes, brushing his mouth with hers. "I love you, my hot cowboy."

Ray froze, and Drew realized what she'd just said.

The words had come out so naturally, without thought. The way truth often did.

Ray looked down at her, green eyes glittering. His chest rose sharply but he was otherwise utterly still.

She expected him at any moment to say something like this was moving too fast, they needed to take a step back, decide where this was going. Which was usually code for, "See ya. Don't call me."

"Yes, I said it." Drew's voice shook. "I'm owning it. Not taking it back."

Ray remained silent as he gazed down at her, not a muscle moving.

Then with a strength that startled her, he dragged Drew against him and gave her a fierce, hot kiss.

He tasted of coffee, passion, anger. Drew sensed pent-up emotions boil to the surface, pouring out of him in a powerful kiss.

Ray lifted her from her feet, cradling her against his hard chest. "Never take it back," he said swiftly. "Never."

They were in the bedroom in a few steps, Ray kicking the door closed. The bed was still messy from their abrupt departure this morning, but it didn't stop Ray from depositing Drew on the bed, stripping her and himself of clothes and making fast and furious love to her.

RAY LAY NEXT TO DREW, WHO WAS AWAKE, BREATHING HARD after their wild ride. They were on top of the blankets, the sunshine enough to keep them comfortable. They'd also just generated a lot of heat.

He'd never met a woman like her.

Drew turned her head on the pillow and caught Ray looking at her. She flushed. "Hi."

"Hey, yourself." Ray moved closer and kissed her, savoring her.

When he finished, he remained on his elbow, gazing down at her. Outside, the real world waited for them to dress and go, to join it again. Ray saw no reason to rush.

"I feel ..." Drew considered. "Decadent."

"Yeah? Is that good?"

Drew's answering smile told Ray all he needed to know. "I've never been decadent before. I always did the responsible thing—went to work, brought home the groceries, made sure my kid had everything she needed." Drew passed fingers over her cheek. "What's happened to me?"

"You abandoned Erica to the Campbells. You'll have to pay for that."

Drew laughed softly. "She's abandoned *me*. Can't wait to rush over there and ride horses with her new friends." She let out a breath. "She's so happy, Ray. I've never seen her this happy."

Ray wiped a tear from her lashes. "And that makes you cry?"

"If you only knew. She had a hard time when her dad died, but she never broke down. But I knew she hurt. And I couldn't make it better. We just slogged on day after day. It wasn't terrible, but it wasn't good either. You know?"

"I think I understand." Day to day life—he got through it,

but it was like walking through molasses sometimes. Lately though, he'd wanted to dance on light feet, like he had last night, with Drew in his arms.

She'd told him she loved him. Right out there in the kitchen. Ray didn't know if she'd been lost in a happy moment or really meant it, and he didn't want to ask to find out.

What if he told her he loved her too? Ray's throat closed up and he lay back down. If he said that, and she laughed at him, it would rip his guts out.

Best be quiet and see how things went.

"You okay?" Drew loomed over him in concern.

Ray rearranged his expression. "With a beautiful naked woman bending over me? I think I'm just fine."

"Goof." Drew rubbed his shoulder playfully.

Ray growled. He pulled her down to him, kissing her and losing himself in her once more.

JULES NEVER CALLED BACK, NOR DID HE SHOW UP IN Riverbend. Drew didn't pursue it, not wanting him to know she knew what he'd done.

Ross Campbell told her he'd checked with his contacts in Chicago, who related that Jules Bolan hadn't left town— was living in his house and going to work every day as usual. Ross had no way of connecting him with the kids who'd vandalized the house except their word, and it was a vague word. Jules, as Drew suspected, hadn't tried to pay his hirelings, so they couldn't trace him through the payment.

Ross said, in a reassuring tone, that he didn't think Jules

would try again once he found out the young men had been caught. Too risky.

Drew didn't quite agree. Jules could be underhanded. But tearing down work she'd spent money on to prevent her from inheriting the B&B showed a vindictiveness she hadn't realized he had. Did he really hate her that much?

Drew heard nothing more from Jules, however, and the work remained undisturbed. Jack and his workers returned, Ray joined them, and the house progressed little by little.

Why she'd decided to tell Ray, loud and clear, that she loved him, she didn't know. Well, she hadn't *decided*. It slipped out. Needed to.

A long time had passed since she'd fallen in love with a man, if she ever had. She'd been infatuated with Philip—she understood that now. Drew hadn't known what honest love felt like until Erica had been put into her arms.

She felt that now for Ray.

But if he wanted to keep it casual, she'd keep it casual. What they had was great. Why mess that up?

She said nothing more about it, and neither did he. He continued to be his hot, wonderful self, and she let things rest there.

October became November, and chilly nights set in. Drew observed with amusement that Riverbenders thought it was cold. But the sun still shone and afternoons could be warm. No snow in sight.

One evening, when the air was crisp, and Thanksgiving and football was on everyone's minds, Ray asked Drew to go with him into town.

Erica was once again with the Campbells. Her riding had progressed, and she was to compete in a local horse show held the week before Thanksgiving, a small event for the kids of River County to show off their skills. Erica was deeply invested in Riverbend now, and Drew hoped to never uproot her again.

Ray said nothing about where they were going as they headed into Riverbend. Drew assumed the diner, but Ray drove past it and parked behind the library.

"This is your big surprise?" Drew asked, sending him a teasing smile. "A night at the library?"

Ray looked mysterious and led her inside.

In a meeting room on the main floor—the room a harmony of polished wood and historic furniture—Drew found a circle of people waiting. Mrs. Ward and Dena, the librarian. Olivia Campbell, the matriarch of the Campbell clan. Mr. Carew, who ran the bank. Mr. Carew sat close to Olivia, the two sharing space that told Drew that if they weren't together, they soon would be.

Mrs. Kaye, the final member of the little group, passed around a tray of cookies. She held the tray out to Drew, beaming a smile.

"So glad you're here, dear. Cookie? Grace made them at her bakery, so you know they'll be extra good."

Drew readily took one—they looked chocolatey and gooey. "Thank you. Is this a book club? What are you reading?"

"No, dear. You sit down over there, with Ray." Mrs. Kaye pointed to two empty chairs. When Drew and Ray obediently took their seats, Mrs. Kaye stood before them, cookie tray dispensed with, hands folded.

"Ray asked us to be here tonight, honey," Mrs. Kaye announced. "We're going to tell you about your grandparents. The truth. I think, looking around the room, that I'm the only one left who knows all of it."

Chapter Seventeen

❧❀❧

D rew didn't have time to be surprised or trepidatious—
Mrs. Kaye launched straight into her tale.

"Now, Miss Paresky, I know these ladies gave you the impression that your father might have been illegitimate. At least, not really a Paresky." She gave Mrs. Ward and Dena a disapproving look. "But they were just girls at the time, and they only remember the gossip. Abby Paresky was my *friend*."

Mrs. Ward looked contrite, a strange thing to see in the formidable woman. Dena frowned, clearly unhappy at being called out.

Mrs. Kaye went on. "Your grandma and I were indeed wild girls, dear. You might laugh about that now, but we had long legs and long hair and we chased handsome men. Caught them too." She smiled in remembered delight. "I was lucky—I met Mr. Kaye and had fun fending him off for a while. Abby, she was never certain what she wanted. She and your grandfather went out from time to time, and she liked him, I could tell. But Lonnie was the settle-down type, and Abby had a hankering to see the world. Can't blame her. In that day and age, women were supposed to get married and have babies as soon as they graduated high school. We even took classes on housekeeping so we'd be ready. Girls were going to college by then, yes, but most of the ones I knew went with the goal of meeting potential husbands. Abby and I planned to change the world, but Riverbend wasn't the place to do it from."

"Times aren't so different," Olivia Campbell broke in. "Girls are still expected to be moms as soon as possible. But there's nothing wrong with having a family."

She spoke with the pride of a matriarch who had five sons and plenty of grandchildren.

"Did I say there was, Livvy Campbell?" Mrs. Kaye demanded. "Mr. Kaye and I did just fine. Love only grows deeper as the years go on—that is, if you choose the right partner in the first place. Abby couldn't ever make up her mind whether Lonnie was the right one or not."

"But she married my grandfather in the end," Drew said.

"She did. After she got pregnant. She let everyone in town believe that the bull rider she'd been going out with—what's his name ... Travis, I think—was the dad. I asked her why, when I knew darn well her baby was Lonnie Paresky's."

"How did you know?" Drew asked. Ray reached over and took one of her hands, his strength comforting. "Did she tell you?"

Mrs. Kaye sent her a pitying look. "Because she never shared a bed with anyone but Lonnie, that's how I knew. She pretended to chase the cowboys, but she always went home alone, or with me, or with Lonnie. Abby was shy, and afraid of being pushed into a life she didn't want. Back then, it was hard for a woman to strike out on her own. Best thing she could do was find a man who wanted the same things she did. Lonnie loved her—would do anything for her."

Drew's eyes stung. "Then why couldn't they make it work out?"

Mrs. Kaye shook her head. "I don't know. Stubbornness, I guess. Pride, and young hearts. When Lonnie found out Abby was pregnant, he was ecstatic. He convinced her to marry him and quickly. You just weren't an unwed mother in those days, especially in this town. She'd have been—what's that word? Excoriated."

Drew nodded, understanding. Her grandmother had faced a difficult time.

"Lonnie thought that once they were a happy family, settled in Riverbend, fixing up the B&B—which Abby loved, by the way—everything would be fine. But Abby still wanted to see the world, to be involved in it, if you know what I mean, while Lonnie was happy to hide himself away and be an innkeeper. Lonnie claimed you could see the world from right here, listening to all the stories the folks who came through told. But when you're twenty and want to roam, you don't want to hear that you'll spend your whole life cooking and cleaning in a B&B. So after a couple years, Abby up and left."

Drew swallowed the lump in her throat. "They wanted different things," she managed to say.

"Lonnie tried to understand, to let her spread her wings," Mrs. Kaye said. "But he was hurt she didn't think he was good enough for her. So they fought."

Mr. Carew leaned forward, speaking in a quiet voice. "Lonnie was a friend. I was a bit younger than he was, and I helped out at the B&B. I want you to understand, Drew, that both your grandparents could be ... well ... pigheaded." He gave her a little smile. "They argued a lot—I heard them—but at the same time, I could tell they loved each other, loved deeply. There was never anyone else for either of them. When she left, Lonnie was angry but also brokenhearted. He never got over it, never stopped trying to win her back."

"He never came to see her," Drew said, torn between sorrow and anger. "I believe you when you say there was no one else for either of them—my grandmother never remarried. But if my grandfather loved her so much, why didn't he show up on her doorstep?"

Mr. Carew shook his head. "Lonnie was a prideful man. He was certain Abby would get her fill of the big city and run back home. He waited. But she never came."

"She found her own life." Drew gently gripped Ray's hand, letting it anchor her. "Raising her son, working at museums. She loved it. But she was lonely—I know she was. I don't know if she ever considered returning to Riverbend. She never talked about it."

Mrs. Kaye cleared her throat. "Abby *was* coming back. She told me. She and Lonnie started communicating again in the last years of her life. He had let the B&B run down once he realized he'd lost Abby for good, but somehow they reconnected. I don't know if she reached out or he did—she wasn't specific. All I know is Lonnie was excited, and he started gussying up the B&B, getting it ready for her return. And then Abby passed away."

Drew blinked back tears. She thought of the signs of previous renovation Ray had found—new plumbing and cleaned-out walls that had been once again neglected.

"He let it go to ruin a second time," Drew said softly. "That was why."

Mrs. Kaye nodded sadly. "When Abby passed on, all the

heart went out of him. Lonnie became a recluse and closed the B&B forever."

Mr. Carew leaned in again. "Lonnie came to me and set up the trust. He knew his son was gone, but he'd learned about you from Abby, knew you were his granddaughter and his heir. He wanted to make sure you came home to Riverbend and fixed up the house, to make it a happy place now that it was too late for him and Abby."

"Too late," Drew echoed, tears trickling to her cheeks. "That's so sad."

Mrs. Kaye broke in briskly. "It is sad. For them. If they'd unbent, admitted they loved each other, and worked it out ..." She trailed off with a sigh. "I loved Abby, I truly did. Mr. Kaye and I tried to make her and Lonnie see reason, to show them how happy *we* were, but you can't run other people's relationships. It's a closed door, no matter how good your intentions are."

"He wants the B&B to be beautiful for her," Drew said. "He wants it to be the home he meant it to be."

"I believe that's true," Olivia said. "But he can't make that choice for you." She gave Drew a wry smile. "Lonnie is still trying to have his own way."

"I think he's trying to make up for the happiness he lost." Drew held more tightly to Ray's hand, liking that he let her work through this, didn't try to tell her what to do or feel. He simply watched her with his fine green eyes, being there for her. "This is the only way he knows how to do it."

Mr. Carew spread his fingers. "It is up to you, Miss Paresky. He set you a hard and expensive task. No one would blame you if you walked away. Someone else will buy the property, no harm done."

Mrs. Kaye didn't agree, Drew could see, but the woman

pressed her lips together and didn't speak. Everyone in the room watched Drew, waiting to see what she'd decide.

"I want to stay," she said softly. "I want to do this. I never sensed my grandmother was unhappy when I grew up—we had fun. But my family never seemed complete. I'd like to complete it—for them."

Mrs. Kaye relaxed into a smile. "You're a sweet young woman, dear. So much like Abby."

"She can't do it alone." Ray gazed at the collected company, a protective bulk at Drew's side. "Mr. Paresky was still a little nuts, if y'all won't take offense. Had grandiose ideas, am I right? So we need to help Drew with this project. Money, time, whatever we all can do. She's one of us now."

"Of course she is." Mrs. Kaye leaned down and wrapped Drew in a peppermint-scented hug. "We'll do whatever it takes, dear. Dena can research whatever you need. Mr. Carew can help you with financial questions, Olivia is already looking after your daughter a lot, and Mabel can keep everyone in pie. Yes, you will," Mrs. Kaye said sternly when Mrs. Ward stirred in her seat. "You and Grace can bake up a storm."

Mrs. Kaye loved the spotlight, Drew could see. Mrs. Kaye beamed at the group, gazed pointedly at Drew's and Ray's entwined hands, and gave them both a wink. "I think that B&B will be the happiest place ever, real soon."

"You okay?"

Ray glanced at Drew as he drove through the darkness to the B&B. She'd said little since they'd left the library.

Drew came out of her reverie. "I'm fine." Her voice was

soft, whispery. "I can't help thinking about how my grand-parents let their lives get away from them. If they hadn't given in to the drama and angst, if they'd met each other halfway ... They could have had so much together."

"Possibly." Ray answered with caution. "You never know, though. So many factors. I agree about the drama." He shot her another glance. "Is that what it was like with your husband?"

"Sort of. He was cold instead of raging, but he turned every situation into a stage for his opinions. As a way to belittle me. That got old."

Probably not fast enough, Ray suspected. Drew was an optimist and tended to give people a chance. Lucky for Ray she did.

"It was drama with me and Christina too. Not really between us, but every time Grant walked into the room ..." Ray shook his head. "I ceased to exist."

Drew didn't answer, and Ray looked over to see her gazing at him steadily.

"What?" he asked.

"I'm trying to imagine how *you* could cease to exist for someone. I like Christina now that I've gotten to know her, but I have to say, she was stupid."

Ray tried a grin. "Well, when we broke up, she did say it was her not me."

"Damn right. It was entirely her." Drew let out a breath. "I guess she was like my grandparents—there was one guy, and it was Grant."

"And I knew that," Ray admitted. "Knew it going in. I wasn't really surprised when she ended it. Not devastated either."

He knew he should shut up, but he wanted Drew to know

he was over Christina. Had been for a long time. Over her even before they broke up.

"I know."

Drew's quiet answer made his heart thump. She did understand—she understood him like no one else had.

He took her hand in his. Ray didn't know what it was about holding hands with her that was so wonderful. Sex was definitely more over-the-top and crazy. But her sliding her fingers through his made him warm all over.

"By the way," she said in her water-smooth voice. "Thanks for tonight. For letting Mrs. Kaye explain. I know you set that up."

"You deserved to know. To tell the truth, a lot of it was Mrs. Kaye's idea. She cornered me at the feed store and said you'd been told the wrong side of the story, and what was I going to do about it?" He chuckled. "I believe her when she says she was wild back in the day."

Drew leaned to him and kissed his cheek. "Thanks, Ray."

They rode in silence for the rest of the drive, and were equally quiet when they entered the empty apartment. They only broke the night's peace with raw cries as they took each other fiercely in the comfort of Drew's bed.

DREW'S LIFE FELL INTO A PLEASANT ROUTINE. A BARRAGE OF workmen would fall on the house in the early morning and labor until late afternoon. Ray worked with them on the days he didn't tend to business at the Malory ranch.

Drew now had school functions with Erica, who had joined the gymkhana team along with Faith. Outgoing Erica had taken well to the school and already had a large circle of friends.

With the help of Dena, Drew did more research on the B&B and Riverbend history, digging out old photos and artifacts with which she'd decorate the house. She also found a friend in Lucy Malory, who accompanied her on buying trips to Austin, helping her pick out fabrics and furniture.

Thanksgiving arrived, and Drew and Erica joined the Malorys, including Dr. Anna, now firmly engaged to Kyle. Grace and Carter came for dessert, bringing Faith and baby Zach with them.

Anna and Kyle would marry in the spring. Wedding planning took up much of the talk at the Thanksgiving table, though the guys soon quietly faded from the dining room.

Drew suggested that since the B&B was coming along so well that Anna and Kyle could have their wedding there in the spring, a week before its grand opening.

Everyone thought this a wonderful idea, which made Drew have nervous second thoughts. She'd been caught up in wedding excitement, and so much could go wrong with the B&B between now and then. But she crossed her fingers and joined in the planning.

Christmas saw Drew and Erica still living over the garage, but in a beautifully refurnished apartment, with a new kitchen, polished floors, and antique furniture that softened up the place. Drew feared Ray would find it too frilly for him, but he didn't seem to mind.

He'd also become a solid part of Drew's life. They never talked about what they had or where they were going—he was simply there, sharing her bed and her dining room, helping work on the house, driving Erica around when Drew couldn't.

Every evening found him at Drew's table with her and Erica. Either Drew would cook, or Ray would make steaks or chicken on the grill he'd bought and set up behind the garage, or he'd take them out to the diner or farther afield to restaurants in Austin or San Antonio.

He stayed over Christmas Eve, and on Christmas morning surprised Erica with a beautiful hand-tooled leather saddle, telling her she should think about getting her own horse. It could be boarded at the Malory or Campbell ranch, no problem. Wouldn't be an expense either, because one of the Malory horses was set to retire from roping, and that horse was very good with kids.

Ray was like a god to Erica after that.

For Drew, Ray had bought a bookcase and filled it with fancy bound editions of Agatha Christie and Dorothy Sayers mysteries.

"Everyone told me to get you jewelry," he said when Drew showered him with thanks and kisses. "But I know you like books."

"Who wouldn't?" Drew exclaimed.

She'd bought *him* a new cowboy hat—in consultation with Kyle—which he studied with admiration. Apparently the brand and style were just right.

After the brief lull of Christmas, work on the house became more frantic, and Drew's worry increased.

What if she couldn't finish in time? Would she have to forfeit the trust? And what would she do then? Jobs weren't thick on the ground in River County, and she and Erica would need income. She might be able to work at the library in town, but Dena had told her in confidence that the county couldn't pay much.

Taking Erica away from Riverbend would break the girl's heart. Drew's too.

The cold of January and February softened to March, spring coming early in the Hill Country. This had been Drew's first winter without snow, which had been strange to her, but she could see where she'd quickly grow used to it.

Most of the ground floor of the B&B had been finished by the end of March, if not furnished, but the second floor bathrooms still needed to be overhauled, not to mention every room upstairs had to be stripped down and re-painted and re-floored.

Anna and Kyle were due to wed soon. The B&B had several downstairs bedrooms ready, though the pair were heading to Hawaii for the honeymoon—"Only place we can find any privacy," Kyle had growled.

Drew needed guests. That was a stipulation of the trust. What if she finished the B&B, spending every penny of the grant and more besides, and no one came to stay?

On a windy morning with the wedding a week away, Drew glanced out the window to see two strangers climb out of a pickup below her apartment.

No, not strangers. They looked familiar.

Ray and the workers were busy inside the house, so Drew went down to see who they were, her heart thumping strangely. She hadn't heard a word from Jules all winter—no Christmas card or gift for Erica this year—but she didn't think he'd given up harassing Drew.

As she stepped outside, a young man with blond hair and a deep tan grinned at her with very white teeth. The slightly older man with him had dark hair and dirt in the creases of his skin, but his smile was just as enthusiastic.

"Hi there," the blond man said, and the dark-haired one nodded.

"Hello," Drew responded politely. "Can I help you?"

"Heard you had rooms to rent."

"Oh." Drew started, then recovered, pretending to be businesslike. "We're not quite open yet, but I do have a couple rooms on the ground floor and one in the basement—all recently renovated. If you want—"

"Great!" the blond man cut her off. "We'll take them. We can bring our gear later today and sign whatever we need to sign. We have funding, don't worry. Credit card and everything."

Drew could hardly say no. "How many—"

"Five of us. Two women and us three guys. So much better than the tents and campers we've been living in. Ray told us about this place and the thought of running water and a roof over our heads ... We couldn't resist."

"Tents?" Drew began, then realized. "Oh, you're the archaeologists ..."

"That's us." The dark-haired man, whose accent put him as originating far from Texas, tipped his baseball cap. "Excavation is hot work. Don't worry, we'll clean ourselves up and leave our pickaxes at the dig." His smiled widened, as though he'd made a good joke.

"All right then," Drew said, trying to remain businesslike and not dance a sudden jig. "The rooms are yours."

"Great," the blond man bounced on his toes. "See you later." Both turned for the truck, then the blond man swung back. "Tell Ray thanks. He's a bud."

"Yes," Drew said as the two happy young men leapt into the pickup and slammed the doors. "Yes, he is."

Chapter Eighteen

✾✾✾

Anna and Kyle's wedding day dawned, a fair and crisp April morning. Anna arrived at the B&B early, a nervous wreck, and let Drew, Grace, and Lucy fuss over her. Or, not so much *let* them as tolerated it.

"You're a beautiful bride, Anna," Lucy said as she smoothed out the wedding gown on the hanger. "Kyle's tongue will be on the floor."

"Eeww," Erica declared. "He might step on it. Lucy's right, though. You're so pretty, Anna."

Anna flushed under their gazes. She did look lovely, Drew thought, giving Anna an impetuous hug. Anna's golden hair, pulled back into a complicated knot Grace had expertly pinned, shone like sunshine.

Lucy wistfully brushed the silk of the ivory gown. She had relaxed a long way since she'd come home, and now assisted Anna in her vet clinic when she wasn't helping Drew put decorative touches on the B&B. She loved animals and had decided to train to be a veterinary assistant. What Anna could pay her was a far cry from what she'd made as a stockbroker in Houston, but that didn't seem to bother her anymore.

Drew had spied Lucy several times during the last six months in the company of Hal Jenkins. She wasn't sure if it was serious, at least on Lucy's part, but Hal was a nice guy, and Drew hoped the best for them.

"This is *your* big day, Drew," Anna said when Drew released her. "I don't want to screw it up for you."

"Big day for *me?*" Drew laughed. "You're the one getting married."

"Yes, but this is your debut." Anna flushed again. "Everyone gets to see what you've done with the B&B. At the grand opening next week, you'll have fulfilled the terms of your grandfather's bequest and inherit all the money. I don't want something stupid at the wedding to drive guests away and force you to close."

"First of all, you worry too much." Drew adjusted the spray of white baby's breath in Anna's hair. "Second, everyone's going to love watching you get married, no matter what happens. You just focus on hot, hot Kyle at the end of the aisle."

Lucy grimaced. "I'm not sure I like to think of my brother as *hot, hot Kyle*. I know he's good-looking, but TMI."

Grace busied herself making ribbon roses. "I second that."

"Mom is thinking of hot, hot Ray." Erica grinned. "She wishes she was the one getting married—to Ray."

All eyes snapped to Drew, two pairs of them Malory green. "Yeah?" Lucy asked. "Is Ray being slow on the uptake?"

"We're not getting married," Drew said, a bit too quickly. "Not even talking about it. Erica is dreaming."

"Oh, come on." Erica folded her arms on the chair she straddled, back to front. "Ray spends a lot of nights over, and he sleeps with you. Don't think I don't know that. Duh."

Drew's face was on fire. "I know, but ... We're taking things slow."

The three ladies exchanged amused glances, Anna looking relieved the focus was off her.

"I'd say dead slow," Lucy said. "Maybe watching Kyle marry Anna today will light a fire under his butt."

Anna appeared skeptical and Grace, ever sensitive to nuance, gave Drew a glance of sympathy. "None of our business, I'm thinking," she said gently.

Lucy snorted. "Since when have our brothers stayed out of *our* business?"

"Good point." Grace put a finishing touch on a bow and found a bobby pin to fix it to Erica's dark hair. "Lovely. When your mom and Ray finally get married, you can be her bridesmaid."

Erica's eyes lit. She was pretty in the slim blue dress she and Drew had chosen for the wedding, so different from the scruffy jeans and cowboy boots she now lived in. She was growing up, Drew thought with a pang. Soon Erica would need a prom dress, and then a wedding dress of her own.

Drew turned quickly away as tears stung her eyes.

"That'd be great," Erica said to Grace. "If I'm not too *old* by then."

The sisters and Anna laughed. Beautiful women together, Drew mused as she joined in the laughter. The three of them happy.

The sound of a door opening made them all jump. Karen entered with her usual flair, no quiet tapping and politely asking admittance.

She wore a white linen dress that bared her arms and

showed a lot of leg, but Drew knew she hadn't been in this outfit when she'd arrived. Drew had watched her roll up with Jack Hillman on his Harley, Karen in jeans and motorcycle boots.

"I hate to interrupt," Karen said without greeting, "but you'd better come." She shot a meaningful look at Drew.

Drew's heart thumped. What had gone wrong? Had the flowers wilted? The arbor collapsed? The musicians gone on strike? Had Kyle passed out and was being rushed to the hospital?

With more and more dire scenarios flashing through her head, Drew hurried with Karen down the stairs and across the full parking area to the house.

The porch, refinished with floorboards painted a dark gray, had been hung with garlands of roses and pink ribbons. The front door, a masterpiece of polished oak, opened to a wide hall that featured the grand staircase.

Restored by Jack's workers and Ray's care, the staircase was magnificent, a song of turned spindles and a gleaming railing that led the eye up to the landing. The window there, full of glistening new glass, let in the bold Texas sunshine.

Drew had been stunned by the hall's beauty when Ray had revealed it to her, but today she hurried through without pausing to admire it, and followed Karen out to the back.

The garden had revealed itself once it had been cleared of weeds, with rows of perennials and bulbs springing into bloom when winter's chill receded. Jack had hired people to fix the watering system—necessary in a climate where rain was unpredictable—and clumps of bluebells, stocks, and roses now filled the green patches with color. The fields around the inn had blossomed, as Ray had assured her they would, with a riot of bluebells turning the ground a shimmering azure.

The arbor was standing just fine, covered in ribbons and more roses. The minister stood by, chatting with Mr. Carew. No one was rushing around in panic. Kyle paced in the garden under Ray's supervision, upright and whole, not on a gurney.

Drew opened her mouth to ask, "What is it?" when Karen led her around the corner of the house.

Drew didn't realize that Erica had followed them until her daughter's voice rang out, "Uncle Jules!"

Jules Bolan waited under a tree a little way from the main garden, deep in shadow, unnoticed. In the distance, Drew heard car doors slamming as more guests arrived, voices surging as the house and garden filled. The sounds dimmed as her ears began to buzz, her focus on Jules.

Erica passed Drew and Karen at a run. Jules, his pale complexion out of place under all the sunshine, straightened up stiffly. He obviously hadn't anticipated that Erica would come out for this meeting.

"You haven't called in forever," Erica said to him. She ceased her mad rush as though sensing he wasn't in the mood for a hug. "I know how to ride a horse now, isn't that cool? I've already won a blue ribbon!"

A true doting uncle would smile and say that was wonderful. Ray and Carter had taken Erica and Faith out for ice cream after that successful show, both girls winning in their classes.

Jules remained rigid. "Erica, I need to talk with your mother."

Erica deflated. "I know what *that* means. I also think I'm old enough to hear some things."

"Not these things." Jules gave Drew a sharp look, with a side glance at Karen, who'd planted herself, arms folded. "Can we speak somewhere private?"

"You gave up that right when you paid people to vandalize my house," Drew snapped.

Jules's lips tightened. "I'd like to see you prove that. I'll call it slander, and my lawyers will make mincemeat of you. All right, if you want your friend and daughter to stay, they can. I want you to sign this piece of property over to me. You can do a quitclaim deed. I've brought the paperwork."

"Why the hell would I do that?" Drew clenched her fists. "Grandfather left this property to *me* and me alone. The trust is clear."

"And it will bring you nothing but hell. A house like this is difficult to maintain, and the idea of you running a bed and breakfast is ludicrous. You'll have guests suing you in no time."

"So I should simply deed the property to you? What will *you* do with it?"

"Sell it," Jules said promptly. "Use the money to take care of Erica. Send her to collage. You don't have a fund for that, do you?"

Jules knew damn well Drew had never been able to afford to put much money aside for Erica's education. She had started a savings account for some of it when Erica had been born, which included gifts from Drew's parents and Philip's. But she'd saved nothing near enough to pay for more than a year at a state college, even if Erica lived at home. Erica had stoutly declared she didn't mind getting a part-time job when she was old enough to help pay for it.

"If I run the B&B as Grandfather wanted me to, I'll

inherit the rest of the legacy," Drew pointed out. "More than enough to pay for Erica to go to college."

"Go to college where? *Here?*" Jules glanced at the open fields behind the B&B in distaste.

"Texas has some of the best universities in the country," Drew began, but Erica interrupted.

"I'm going to Texas A&M, like Dr. Anna. I'm going to be a vet!"

"No, you are not," Jules declared, which was exactly the wrong thing to say. When Erica got an idea in her head, she followed it through to its bitter end ... unless she changed her mind. Drew had learned to let her dreams play out.

Erica's expression turned stubborn. "Why not?"

"You'll never get anywhere in a school like that," Jules said dismissively. "We'll talk about it later."

Erica looked mulish. "I want to talk about it *now.*"

"Erica." Drew kept her voice quiet, so quiet that Erica glanced at her in surprise. Erica had learned to assess her mother's moods, though, and closed her mouth, though she wasn't subdued.

"You can't control her, can you?" Jules had the bad habit of talking about Erica as though she couldn't hear him. "She's turning into a brat. Her dad wouldn't like that."

The best way for Jules to upset Erica was to talk about Philip. Drew knew he did it on purpose.

Drew put herself between him and Erica. "Time for you to go, Jules. This is *my* home. The only reason you want your hands on this land is that it's worth a lot of money. Karen explained it to me—this is prime property, close to Austin, ready for a big developer to swallow. If I quitclaim it to you, I get nothing for it, but you can sell it for millions."

Jules glanced at Karen, tried his belittling gaze, and then looked uncertain. Karen stared him down like a basilisk.

"What does *she* know?" Jules said. "Backwoods real estate woman."

"You're cute, honey," Karen said in cool amusement. "You remind me of my second husband. He was a total bastard."

Drew planted her fists on her hips. "I know you, Jules. You'd turn around and sell this property to the highest bidder. Then run back home with your cash while the bulldozers tear the land to shreds and pop identical flimsy houses onto it. Why should you care? This is a small town, a blip on your radar. But it's my *home*. My grandparents' home. I have friends here, and I'm not going to see their town become another faceless housing development."

Jules scowled. "You're an incompetent woman and a bad mother. I can prove both. You give this property to me and go back home, and I won't send child protective services down on your hide. You've totally ruined my brother's daughter, and I will never forgive you for that."

Drew took a step toward him. She sensed someone behind her, a heat she knew meant Ray, ready to protect her.

But even if Ray hadn't been at her back, she knew she was finished with Jules. She understood now that Jules had torn Drew down at every opportunity, chipping away at her confidence, playing on her guilt. She should have banished Jules from their lives long ago, but she'd been reluctant to cut Erica's last tie with her father.

"What you can't forgive was that Philip married me," Drew said in a low but fierce voice. "We were young and in love. We had a lot of fun together—until after the wedding. Then he began to change. He regretted marrying me and didn't fight our separation too hard. For a long time I wondered what was wrong with *me* that Philip found fault in everything I did.

"But I figured it out a while back. It had nothing to do with *me*—it was *you*—I wasn't good enough for you. My roots were in a little Texas town, and my mom was just an ordinary person, not from an old family or old money, or whatever you think she ought to have been. I brought nothing to the marriage but myself. And that wasn't good enough for your precious baby brother. How long did you harangue him to change me to your taste?

"Then when he died, you blamed *me*. Never mind he was driving to Milwaukee to see his girlfriend. So you decided, with your twisted sense of right and wrong, to try to take Erica from me. That was you trying to save your biological relation from the horror that is me and my family. You don't give a shit what *she* wants. Don't pretend what you want for Erica has anything to do with love."

Drew ran out of breath. She became aware of more people around them, not only Ray but Kyle, the Campbell men and their wives, Olivia and Mr. Carew, Mrs. Ward and Dena. Faith came with Carter and Grace, and the girl moved to stand shoulder-to-shoulder with Erica. Dominic, face fixed in the expression of the tough boy he'd had to be, stood on her other side.

Erica had tears on her face, but she didn't break down. She stood tall, head high, and Drew's heart swelled with pride.

Jules regarded Drew coldly, as though her outburst was not unexpected. "You didn't deserve Philip. You're right that you weren't good enough for him. He could have had anyone he wanted, but you latched on to him and twined him around your fingers. Then you dumped him like he was nothing. You don't deserve this property—yes, it is prime real estate. And I can take it away from you. Like that." Jules snapped his fingers. "And I will."

"Like hell you will."

The low drawl came from Ray. He moved forward only a pace, but his presence was enough to make Jules take a small step back.

"Who are *you?*" Jules tried to sound derisive, but the squeak in his voice ruined it.

"A friend." Ray fixed a hard green gaze on Jules. "And you're not doing anything to mess with Drew or her home."

Jules wet his lips. "I'll do what I damn well please."

"No." Ray folded his arms. "You'll get off her property and not come back. You won't go anywhere near her ever again, or her daughter."

Jules shot Ray a furious look. "Erica's not your child."

"Or yours." Ray didn't raise his voice—he didn't have to. "Let me explain so you understand. You aren't going anywhere near Drew, or Erica, because you'd have to come through *me*, and no way am I letting you do that."

Karen gave Jules an icy smile. "And come through me. The lawyers I know are legendary."

"And me," Faith said. "I'm Erica's friend."

"And I think all the rest of us." Kyle stepped next to Ray, the Malory brothers a formidable wall.

The Campbell brothers formed a second wall. Adam, Tyler, Carter, and Grant, the four who'd made it possible for Drew to obtain the funds to work on the B&B, and Ross, the now-elected sheriff who wasn't looking too happy at this stranger in his county. Jack Hillman and Hal stood next to Ross, two large and dangerous men.

They'd all been there for her, she realized, since day one.

The Campbell wives, helping out Drew, and giving Erica a place to find sanctuary and a chance to discover her love of horses. Jack, with his crew who did the grunt work on the house, Manny Judd, who'd eagerly helped take down the vandals trying to destroy her home. Dr. Anna, who was the first to befriend Drew and Erica and doctor their cat. Grace, Lucy, and Kyle, who'd accepted Drew as one of the family. Karen, who'd convinced the Campbell brothers to give Drew the grant, and bestowed sensible, if pointed, advice. Mrs. Kaye, who'd helped Drew understand her grandparents' past and their love and sadness.

Drew worked on the house not only for her grandparent's sake, making it the happy home they'd wanted, but also for herself. This was *her* place, *her* work, *her* life.

But she couldn't have done it without the amazing people from Riverbend.

Her grandfather had known that, she realized. He'd known his town had a large heart, and would help her at every turn. He'd been a wise man, in his way.

"You know what, Jules?" Drew said, an ease flowing into her heart. "You're done here. This is my home now—*this* is my family." She waved at her collected friends. "And they're one hundred percent better than you and what you think is important. They embraced me, they *helped* me, while you stood back and waited for me to fail. Well, I won't fail, because all these people have my back, and I have theirs. That's what *real* family is, Bolo."

Jules glanced at the people edging closer to him, and his face grew even more pale. "You've always been a loser, Drew *Paresky*." He spit the name. "You *owe* me."

"She owes you nothing." Ray's quiet voice cut through

Jules's rage. "Now, my brother's about to get married. I'd say it's time for you to go."

Kyle, resplendent in a tux and cowboy boots, nodded. "Yep. I'd hurry, before my wife-to-be comes looking for me. She knows how to castrate."

Jules puffed up. "Are you threatening..."

"No." Ross Campbell stepped toward him, his brothers closing ranks behind him. "I'm the sheriff of this here little county you're dissing, and I'm asking you to leave it. Drew's free to file a restraining order if she wants, but right now, I can tell you to get out or cool off in my lockup. Sanchez is on duty, a little annoyed he drew the short straw and can't make the wedding. I imagine he's a little cranky."

"I'm not breaking any laws," Jules said hotly.

"You're trespassing," Ross said. "We take that seriously in Texas."

"I'll see you—"

Drew pushed past Ray and Ross and stared Jules down. "Just go."

Something in her face convinced Jules at last. He met her gaze for a brief moment and then couldn't look at her anymore.

Jules shrugged, his face tight, pretending to the last that leaving was his decision.

He turned and made for his car, and the whole town walked with him. Jules didn't offer any eye contact as he slid into the driver's seat of his Mercedes and started it up. He made a show of putting on his seatbelt and adjusting the mirror before he tried to smoothly pull out.

The purring car clanked as Jules drove over a big rock, but it righted itself and glided down the drive in a cloud of dust.

"Good riddance!" Erica's shout rose. Her face shone with tears, and she had her arms folded tightly, but her grin broke through.

Drew leaned to her and pulled her into a tight embrace. "Honey, I'm so sorry you had to see that."

"Don't worry, Mom." Erica's voice was muffled as she hugged Drew back. "I never liked him much. I only was nice to him because of you."

Drew wasn't certain she believed that, but Erica was sweet to try to make her feel better.

"I love you, Erica."

"Love you too, Mom."

Ray was right beside them. Erica turned and flung her arms around his neck. "Love you too, Ray!" She planted a noisy kiss on his cheek then caught Faith's hand and Dominic's and ran with them toward the garden.

Ray slid his arm around Drew, his strength keeping her to her feet. "You're beautiful," he said into her ear. "I love you. But you know that."

Drew took a shaking breath, shocked out of her senses by his words. *I love you. But you already know that.* Did she?

This man had been there for her from the beginning, from her first attempt to assess the wreck of her house to making Erica comfortable with Riverbend, to finding Drew the money for repairing the B&B, to sending her the first guests so she'd fulfill all the terms of the trust. He'd done all that for her, for no gain for himself.

No one would do that without love in his heart.

Before Drew could respond to this newfound joy, a rustle of fabric and the voice of Dr. Anna broke through the excited chatter and laughter that accompanied Jules's exit.

"Am I getting married?" Dr. Anna demanded. "Or what?"

Chapter Nineteen

❧❀❧

Ray watched his brother still as he beheld Dr. Anna in her form-hugging wedding gown. White fabric skimmed Anna's body, the skirt widening below her knees to show frothy stuff underneath as she marched down the porch steps. Kyle stared at her, entranced, the stunned disbelief that he actually got to marry her evident.

Lucy dashed out of the house behind Anna. "It's bad luck for the groom to see the bride before the wedding." She cupped her hands around her mouth. "Look away, Kyle."

Kyle drew a breath, his slack jaw tightening. "Screw that." He surged forward past the crowd and Anna's ladies trying to stop him and took Anna by both hands. "Come on, baby. We're starting this thing."

Anna flushed, her happiness showing in her glow. Ray watched them flow into each other as they walked, heads together, Kyle grinning to Anna's laughter.

Kyle needed someone to love him hard, and Anna needed Kyle's easy support. Nice that they'd found each other at last.

The wedding guests drifted toward the folding chairs set

up in front of the arbor, excitement and anticipation in the
air. Hal, looking out of place in a dark suit, went to Lucy in
her bridesmaid's gown and offered his arm. Lucy, flushing,
took it.

Yeah, that was going somewhere. Good. Lucy needed
someone strong who liked her for herself.

Karen headed straight for Jack without compunction,
rising on high-heeled tiptoes to kiss his lips. Instead of
looking embarrassed, hard-edged Jack smiled, slid his arm
around Karen, and led her away.

Drew lingered, and finally, she and Ray were alone,
shaded by the big live oak Jules had tried to hide under. Even
the tree hadn't liked him.

"Gotta wonder." Ray gestured at the guests taking seats as
Kyle and Anna separated, Anna moving to the back and
hugging her father who would walk her down the aisle. "Did
all these people come to see what we'd done with the B&B,
or to make sure Kyle marries her?"

"Both." Drew smiled.

Something in her had changed in the last ten minutes.
Ray saw a new strength, a confidence that had come from
ripping her brother-in-law a new one.

She stepped closer. "So, you love me, do you, Ray
Malory?"

Ray's face heated, but he wasn't ashamed. "Sure do."

"It's just ... you've never said it before."

"I haven't?" Ray thought back through the months, weeks,
and days since he'd met Drew. "I fell in love with you a while
back. I think when you dumped drywall compound all over
me at Fuller's store."

"I think that's when I fell in love with you too." Drew's
voice went soft. "When you told me not to worry and helped

me bring all the stuff home. I thought I'd never met such a beautiful man."

"Too bad we didn't know," Ray said, his voice as quiet.

"We were both too scared to say anything. I didn't want to push you, just wanted to see what happened."

"Same here." Drew nodded wistfully. "I was afraid you'd vanish the minute we started talking about a relationship."

"I was afraid *you* would. I wanted you in my life so bad, I didn't want to drive you away. Maybe that's why I never said the words. They were in my head, but I worried what would happen when they came out of my mouth."

"I told *you*." Drew's red lips curved. "Remember? That day after we caught the vandals? I called you *My Hot Cowboy* and then we made amazing love."

"I remember." Every part of Ray's body remembered. "Why do you think I was so quick to get you in that bedroom?"

"You liked your new nickname?"

"The most beautiful woman in the world had just told me she loved me." Ray took her hands and pulled her close. "I love *you*, Drew. I should have said it before, so many times. I was still scared of losing you, I guess. But to hell with that. I'm going to say it now, every day. That okay with you?"

"I think so. Okay if I say I love you too?"

"Yeah." Ray cupped her face. "You say it as much as you want."

He kissed her. Ray tasted the new self-assurance in her, felt it. Her lips were soft, pliant, and yet strong—she'd always been strong. Drew moved her hands down his arms to his waist, then, the tree shielding them, to his backside.

"Ray Malory," she whispered as the kiss ended. "Will you marry me?"

Ray jerked, heart beating wildly. He stepped back, gazing, shocked, into her beautiful, serene blue eyes.

"Oh, hell no."

Drew's softness vanished in an instant. "No?" she repeated numbly.

"I mean *yes*." Ray cupped her shoulders. "I mean ... You aren't supposed to ask me. I had it planned for after the grand opening. Taking you to Chez Orleans, maybe a drive afterward to the river under the stars. Telling you I want to be with you forever, and giving you the velvet box with the ring. I already have the ring—safe at home."

Drew stared at him, stunned, her chest rising with a sharp breath. Her mouth opened and closed a few times before she found words. "So, you were going to—"

"Propose, yep. Pop the question. I was waiting until all this craziness stopped, no weddings, no grand openings. Just the two of us."

Drew's smile began to blossom again, spreading across her face, her eyes shining with it. "Damn. I ruined it."

"No, I'd say you told me how you'll answer." Ray tugged her abruptly against him. "Gives me more confidence. But if you don't want the fancy dinner, the drive under the stars ..."

"Oh, I'll take it." Drew's smile became a grin of delight. "Tell you what. You answer *this* proposal, and then you can do one of your own. Who says it only has to be one of us doing the asking?"

"All right." Dimly Ray heard the wedding's music starting, knowing he needed to be next to his brother when Anna walked down the aisle. "Well, go ahead. Ask me again."

Drew rested her fingers on his chest. "Ray Malory. Will you marry me?"

"Damn right I will." Ray pulled her closer. "I love you, Drew. Love you forever."

Her answering kiss held joy, Ray's blood hot with love and need. He ran hands down her back, bared by the bridesmaid's gown, feeling her supple body rising to his.

The music swelled louder. Drew eased from the kiss, laughing into his mouth. "We'd better get to the wedding before your sisters come and drag us there."

Ray brushed back a lock of her beautiful, silken hair. "Yeah, my sisters are pushy. But they love you too." He took her hand. "Ready to go?"

"With you? Sure am." Drew gave him her sweetest smile.

Ray wished the entire wedding and guests would evaporate, or at least freeze in time, while he ran upstairs with Drew and showed her just how much he loved her. Multiple times, in fact.

Drew squeezed his hand, and he read in her eyes that she wanted him too. "Later," she whispered, and Ray's body hummed in anticipation.

Ray led Drew out from under the tree, the two of them breaking into a run toward the waiting crowd, who'd turned to watch them with interest. Kyle gave his brother a wide grin and a thumbs-up.

Drew parted from Ray to gather with the bridesmaids, a warm Texas wind springing up to flutter the ribbons tied along the B&B's porch and the flowers in her hair.

Epilogue

A week later, the entire town returned as Drew and Ray unveiled the newly renamed Bluebonnet Inn Bed and Breakfast.

Drew stood on the shady side porch overlooking the garden and fields beyond. People wandered into and out of the house, allowed into any room today except those already occupied by guests.

The archaeologists had taken up residence. They were a casual bunch, now lounging on the front porch in shorts and T-shirts, happily drinking the iced tea Erica brought them. Even before the B&B had been finished, they'd loved the place, and were grateful for a place to bathe and sleep.

Drew had already been getting calls for reservations, as the word spread about the lovely restored home in the field of bluebonnets. Erica had named the inn in her rapture at the flowers, and Drew had decided the name a good one.

Ray came out of the cool house and leaned on the porch railing next to her. Together they watched Faith, Erica, and Dominic play a game that involved much running and yelling. So nice that they could be safe and young and oblivious to the darker world.

"Good party," Ray said in his laconic way. "I'm hearing lots of compliments on the house. I'm trying to look modest."

Drew wasn't surprised about the compliments. "You and Jack and crew did a hell of a job."

"You were a good manager," Ray said generously. "Telling us what to do like a drill sergeant."

"Gee, thanks."

"I meant it as a compliment."

Drew grinned and bumped her body into his. "You are such a shit."

"You betcha." Ray continued his scrutiny over the guests milling below. Callie Jones-Campbell wandered slowly by on Ross's arm, her belly round with their first child—expected in June.

"Ever think about having more kids?" Ray asked.

"Mmm. Possibly." Drew had thought a lot about it, in fact, though she kept her voice neutral. The idea of holding a child in her arms who gazed at her with Ray's green eyes was intoxicating.

"Well, I have." Ray covered her hand with his. "No holding back about what I think this time. I'd love to have kids with you. I've even discussed it with Erica. She rolled her eyes, told me she wanted a little brother and that we should hurry up and get on with it."

Drew laughed softly. "Well, no worrying about her then."

"Nope." Ray went silent a moment. "Erica's a good kid."

"She is."

Another pause, while the voices of friends and family drifted to them.

"Then it's all settled," Ray said. "I'll propose to you this

Saturday night, we'll get married this summer, and then we'll make a baby."

"You are so organized."

Ray broke into chuckles. "It's fun to pretend. How about we let the kid come when it does? We're going to be busy running this place anyway."

Ray had never said anything directly, but Drew knew he'd be alongside her every step of the way as she started her new business. With this opening, she'd fulfilled the terms of the trust. Her lawyer had already started the procedure to give her access to the rest of her grandfather's money.

"That's true," Drew said. "Very busy."

"We'll have to take every opportunity to try for a little one."

Drew's body heated. "Sounds like fun."

Again they fell silent, the breeze cooling the soft April air.

Ray put his arm around her, enclosing her in his warmth. "We're not letting anyone up in the apartment today, right?"

Drew glanced at the windows over the garage, her temperature rising every moment. Out in the garden, Erica shrieked with laughter and chased her two best friends. In the shadows of a big tree, Lucy and Hal Jenkins came together in a long kiss.

"Yeah, I see them," Ray said, breath warming her ear. "It's a good thing."

Under the tree, Lucy's body was relaxed, the smile she sent Hal when they parted telling.

"The apartment's off limits, yes," Drew said. "Since we're still living there."

Which meant it would be empty at this moment. No eyes were on them. Ray took Drew's hand and led her down the porch steps and at a quick walk to the garage. Up the stairs, into the apartment, door closed and locked. Drew let out a breath. Made it.

She took another quick breath as Ray began stripping off his shirt. His gorgeous body came into view, powerful and hard-muscled, tanned where he'd worked in the sun. Drew scrabbled with her own clothes, shivering in delight when Ray helped skim off her shirt, then bra.

They dashed into the bedroom, Ray's jeans and Drew's skirt coming off, underwear landing somewhere.

Drew went tight with anticipation as Ray took her down to the bed, his kisses, his touch, lighting everything good inside her. She couldn't keep her hands off him, stroking his skin, fingers in his hair, kissing his lips.

She let out a groan as Ray slid into her, thick with wanting. Her last coherent thought before passion took her was that she was the luckiest woman in the world. She was in a bed in her very own home, while a beautiful cowboy with intense green eyes made hard and fast love to her.

Outside the window, laughter filled the spaces that had so long been silent, and happiness pushed away the last sigh of sad loneliness.

The house and Riverbend had done the same for her.

Thanks, Grandfather. Drew let the thought drift into the sunshine, then pulled Ray down to her and gave into the fire.

"I love you, my hot cowboy," she whispered.

Ray's breath caught. "Love you too, Drew. Sweet angel."

His words filled all the empty spaces, and Drew was complete.

Author's Note

Thank you for reading!

If you've read Kyle's book (*Riding Hard: Kyle*) you'll note that some of the action of *Ray* takes place simultaneously with *Kyle*. I thought it would be fun to introduce Ray's heroine in Kyle's book, and then show in Ray's own book what he was up to when he disappeared from that story. Also, I liked looking at Anna's and Kyle's courtship from a different perspective.

I hope you enjoyed this stay in Riverbend!

BEST WISHES,

Jennifer Ashley

Also by Jennifer Ashley

Bear Attraction

Mate Bond

Lion Eyes

Bad Wolf

Wild Things

White Tiger

Guardian's Mate

Red Wolf

Midnight Wolf

Tiger Striped

A Shifter Christmas Carol

Iron Master

Shifter Made ("Prequel" short story)

Historical Romances

The Mackenzies Series

The Madness of Lord Ian Mackenzie

Lady Isabella's Scandalous Marriage

The Many Sins of Lord Cameron

The Duke's Perfect Wife

A Mackenzie Family Christmas: The Perfect Gift

The Seduction of Elliot McBride

The Untamed Mackenzie

The Wicked Deeds of Daniel Mackenzie

Scandal and the Duchess

Rules for a Proper Governess

About the Author

New York Times bestselling and award-winning author Jennifer Ashley has written more than 100 published novels and novellas in romance, urban fantasy, mystery, and historical fiction under the names Jennifer Ashley, Allyson James, and Ashley Gardner. Jennifer's books have been translated into more than a dozen languages and have earned starred reviews in *Publisher's Weekly* and *Booklist*. When she isn't writing, Jennifer enjoys playing music (guitar, piano, flute), reading, hiking, and building dollhouse miniatures.

More about Jennifer's books can be found at
http://www.jenniferashley.com

To keep up to date on her new releases, join her newsletter here:
http://eepurl.com/47kLL